The Bug Funeral

The Bug Funeral

Sarah R. Shaber

This Large Print edition is published by Thorndike Press®, Waterville, Maine USA and by BBC Audiobooks, Ltd, Bath, England.

Published in 2004 in the U.S. by arrangement with St. Martin's Press, LLC.

Published in 2004 in the U.K. by arrangement with Robert Hale Limited.

U.S. Hardcover 0-7862-6711-9 (Mystery)
U.K. Hardcover 1-4056-3050-7 (Chivers Large Print)
U.K. Softcover 1-4056-3051-5 (Camden Large Print)

A Professor Simon Shaw Mystery

This is a work of fiction. Any resemblance to actual persons, institutions, or events is entirely coincidental.

The text of this Large Print edition is unabridged.
Other aspects of the book may vary from the original edition.

Set in 16 pt. Plantin by Al Chase.

Printed in the United States on permanent paper.

British Library Cataloguing-in-Publication Data available

Library of Congress Cataloging-in-Publication Data

Shaber, Sarah R.
The bug funeral / Sarah R. Shaber.
p. cm.
ISBN 0-7862-6711-9 (lg. print : hc : alk. paper)
1. Shaw, Simon (Fictitious character) — Fiction.
2. History teachers — Fiction. 3. College teachers — Fiction. 4. North Carolina — Fiction. 5. Reincarnation — Fiction. 6. Infanticide — Fiction. 7. Large type books.
I. Title.
PS3569.H226B84 2004
813′.54—dc22 2004047227

For my dear parents,
Frances Purvis Rock and Frank D. Rock, Sr.

Acknowledgments

I want to thank Billy Griffin, president of the alumni association of the former Methodist Home for Children in Raleigh, for inviting me to attend the annual Easter reunion of orphanage alumni in Raleigh, and all the alumni there who told me stories about growing up at the Methodist Home. I emphasize here that none of the people whom I describe in this book really lived at the Methodist Home, and none of the events really happened there. The Raleigh Christian Orphanage is solely a product of my literary imagination.

I also want to thank Joe Freed, manager of Oakwood Cemetery, for the tour and for answering my many questions.

As always, I am so grateful for the help and support of the librarians of Wake County, especially Dale Cousins, Sue Scott, Elena Owens, and Janet Morley. What would all us writers and readers do without you!

After reading this book, some of you might be interested in exploring current research on reincarnation, past-life recollections, past-regression therapy, cryptoamnesia, and Dr. Ian Stevenson's work with children's memories. I would recommend reading *Old Souls: Compelling Evidence from Children Who Remember Past Lives* by Thomas Shroder. The Web sites for *The Straight Dope*, *The Reincarnation FAQ*, and *Skeptic Magazine* also contain interesting information.

1

> Life is infinitely stranger than anything which the mind of man could invent. We would not dare to conceive the things which are really commonplaces of existence.
>
> — SHERLOCK HOLMES TO DR. WATSON

"I remember a past life," she said.

"Really," Simon said. He stopped taking notes, put his pen down, and assumed his best professorial attitude, leaning back in his chair, hands steepled under his chin. He gave the impression he was pondering what she had said, but he was really wondering how soon he could get Helen Williams out of his office. Of all the requests for his expertise he'd received lately, and he'd gotten plenty after the publicity from his last investigation, this was definitely the weirdest.

"You don't have to be polite," she said. "I know what you're thinking. It doesn't bother me anymore. I'm used to it." She kneaded the shallow frown lines in her forehead with the fingers of both hands. "Dr. Ferrell did say you'd help me. I can pay you, too."

Simon was annoyed. What was Ferrell thinking, referring this woman to him? He owed the man a favor, several of them, in fact, but how was he supposed to deal with this nonsense?

"Money is not an issue," Simon said.

"I suppose you don't believe in reincarnation?" she asked.

"No," Simon said. "No, I don't."

"Good," she said. "Neither do I."

"I don't understand why you're here, then."

"Ever since I was a child, I've been haunted by memories of a past life. I've done my best to suppress them. I've gone to psychiatrists, psychologists, even a hypnotist and a medium, you name it. I'm at my wit's end. My boyfriend gets back from a tour of duty in the Middle East in a month. He wants us to get married. That just makes the nightmares worse because he doesn't know this about me, and I'm afraid to tell him."

"What kind of nightmares?"

"My memories of this so-called other life exist alongside my memories of this life. And one of them, well, you see, I remember killing a child, or at least I remember burying it, and I think that I must have killed it. When I'm stressed out about anything, I have nightmares reliving it. Every night."

"How awful for you."

"Wade, Dr. Ferrell, is my godfather. He was my father's college roommate. He suggested I ask you for help. He said that you're a famous historian. That you could find out if I really did live in the past, if anyone can."

She leaned toward him eagerly. "You see, if I could just know, I could accept anything. If I existed in an earlier life, I could deal with that. If I didn't, I'll know there's a psychological explanation for the memories and I'll cope with that, too."

Simon felt a little less dismayed. Wade Ferrell had been his doctor and friend for years. Surely he wouldn't get involved in something that hinted at the occult, or even more troubling, dangerous psychological instability. Helen seemed intelligent and educated, not at all mentally disturbed. She was attractive, too. Despite the tiny frown lines and crow's feet that matured her face, she appeared to be in her late twenties. She wore her dark brown hair in a shoulder-length blunt cut with wispy bangs. She had intense blue eyes and dressed simply in black trousers, a coral sweater, and black clogs. Her handbag and leather jacket were slung over the back of her chair.

"Are you going to help me?" she asked.

"I'll do what I can," Simon said. "When did you, do you think, you lived? Do you know your, uh, name?"

She smiled at him, a wide, amused smile.

She leaned forward in her chair, her hands gripping the arms of her chair, her tension obvious. "Here we go. My name was Annie Evans, and I believe I lived here in Raleigh around nineteen hundred. At least, from my surroundings in the memories, that's what I figure. I took care of children, but not in a home. There were too many of them. A boarding school, maybe."

Distantly, a bell rang.

"I've got to go to class," Simon said, as relieved as he had ever been in his life to close a conversation. "We need to meet again when I have more time. Where can I reach you?"

She wrote a phone number in a little memo book she took out of her purse, tore out the page, and handed it to him. "The hotel's on Hillsborough Street, near N.C. State."

Helen's hotel was a few blocks away from Simon's house in Cameron Park, too, but he didn't mention it. Who knew? She might show up at his door at midnight, with a Ouija board and a crystal ball. Simon walked her to the door of his office. She paused there, waiting for him to speak. When he didn't, she added, "When do you think I might hear from you? I'm a teacher, so I've got Christmas break off, but then I'll have to go back to Wilmington."

"I'll call you this afternoon, after my classes are over."

"Thank you," she said, shaking his hand before she left his office.

Lord, Simon thought to himself, what have I gotten myself into, and how am I going to get out of it?

Simon sat back down at his desk to think. He didn't actually have class now. He'd used the bell as an excuse to end a disturbing conversation.

Simon Shaw was Professor of History at Kenan College, a small liberal arts college in the historic part of downtown Raleigh, North Carolina. Despite his youth, he'd already made a name for himself. His first book, *The South Between the World Wars*, won a Pulitzer Prize and cinched tenure for him several years earlier than was customary. Then there was his detecting. By chance he'd come upon and solved three murders, cold cases that were decades old. It wasn't an avocation he had sought intentionally, but he had been called a forensic historian in the press often enough by now that he had accepted the term himself. Nothing that he had investigated so far, from an heiress gone missing seventy-five years ago to an aging prison inmate who insisted he was innocent of a murder he'd once confessed to, had prepared him for a request like this. He couldn't ignore it because Wade Ferrell had sent Helen Williams to him. Simon looked at his watch. Ferrell had a busy family practice, but it was almost lunchtime so perhaps he could catch him with a few minutes free to talk.

As soon as Simon identified himself to Ferrell's receptionist, she called the doctor to the telephone.

"What is wrong with you?" Simon asked. "I'm not a psychologist."

"Helen doesn't need any more psychologists, she needs a professional historian who can help her find out if her memories are real or imagined. She's a good person, and she needs your help desperately."

"Hell, Wade, you don't believe her!"

"I've known Helen since she was a little girl. I'm her godfather. She's high-strung and imaginative, but she's not crazy. And the memories feel authentic to her, even though she doesn't believe in reincarnation. She's come to a critical place psychologically — if she can't put all this behind her, I don't know what she'll do."

"You want me to find out if a woman named Annie Evans lived in Raleigh almost a hundred years ago?"

"I know it's a lot to ask, Simon, but I've done you a few favors, you know."

"I remember. I'll do what I can."

"That's all I ask."

Simon cradled his phone and thought about what Ferrell had told him. The doctor was one of the most pragmatic people he knew. If he said this woman wasn't disturbed, except for her unusual memories, of course, then she wasn't. And he did owe Ferrell a favor.

Now was not a good time for him to take on a project like this, what with exams and the holidays, but he could manage it. A lot depended on what information Helen could give him about the woman she thought she once was. At least there wasn't a moldering old corpse involved in this case. Not a real one, anyway.

Simon left his office and went down the stairs and across the long, wood-paneled first-floor hall of the history department toward the faculty lounge. The plastic evergreens and holly that twined down the hand-carved oak banister were a bit dusty, but still festive. Twinkly white lights edged the door of the lounge. Emanating from inside was the wonderful odor of Christmas. In a desperate attempt to avoid overeating, the faculty brought in whatever holiday food they had left over from parties and gifts, hoping someone else would eat it. Yesterday, Simon feasted on country ham biscuits, cheese straws, and a hot mug of spiked apple cider for lunch. Simon weighed one hundred and thirty pounds sopping wet after dinner, so he didn't hesitate to eat whatever was available.

Half a pecan pie, a coconut cake, and an open box of homemade chocolate candy called to him from one of the old scarred library tables that furnished the lounge. Fresh coffee dripped into the pot of the staff coffeemaker. This suited Simon just fine. He had no problem with eating dessert for lunch.

He filled a paper plate with food and poured himself a mug of coffee, which he loaded with sugar and milk from a nearby refrigerator, tucked behind a screen plastered with tattered memos and notices.

"I don't want to be around when you fall

off that sugar high this afternoon," Marcus Clegg said from the battered leather sofa upon which he sprawled, tapping on his laptop computer.

"The cure for that is more sugar," Simon said, "carefully spread out over the day to sustain high blood-sugar levels."

"Shouldn't be difficult. There's plenty more in the office. Dr. Jones brought platefuls back from the trustees' party for department chairs last night."

"Please tell me Walker didn't announce his retirement."

"We've been spared another year."

"Thank you, Lord!"

Simon's gratitude sent heavenward was for the continued health and long tenure of Dr. Walker Jones, chair of the history department. Walker Jones taught eighteenth-century American history. He'd been working for years on an Alexander Hamilton biography, hampered by the action of Hamilton's widow, who had burned a trunkful of papers after her husband's death, worried that evidence of Hamilton's philandering would survive for posterity.

Simon admired Jones, but that wasn't the only reason he wanted him to stay. Jones' successor might be Dr. Vera Thayer, the most unpopular professor in the department. If Walker retired at sixty-five or so, Vera would pounce on the chair's job like a duck on a June bug. Vera had the brownie points to succeed Walker as chair: She'd published several books, served on innumerable college and professional committees, and was one of the first women faculty members at Kenan. Walker and Vera were of an age. If Walker retained the chair until the college's maximum retirement age, seventy-two, Vera would probably retire before he did and drive off into the sunset to explore America in her Airstream trailer with her husband and two dachshunds. Simon could only hope.

"Where is Vera today?" Simon asked.

"She was here long enough to complain about the food in the lounge, for the umpteenth time. She said it was unprofessional and attracted bugs. Jack and Sophie were here, too."

Jack Kingfisher was the new assistant professor of American history, specializing in Native American issues and the Civil War. Simon, who had chaired the search committee that recruited Jack, wanted someone who wouldn't parrot the hoary Southern position on slavery, secession, and reconstruction. Jack, a North Carolinian of Cherokee heritage, did a great job walking the fine line between Southern sensibilities and revisionist history. This was crucial at a small Southern college like Kenan, where most of the students had been raised to believe that slavery wasn't the cause of the Civil War.

Sophie Berelman was a very pregnant assistant professor who taught modern European history. Documenting the Holocaust was her research interest. She was determined to interview every Holocaust survivor she could find in North Carolina. There were a surprising number, and the clock was ticking. World War II was rapidly receding into the distant past, and soon few people would be alive who had experienced it personally.

Marcus yawned, stretching his hands above his head. "So what have you accomplished this morning? I saw an attractive woman entering your office awhile ago."

"You wouldn't believe me if I told you," Simon said.

"New girlfriend, I hope?" Marcus said.

Marcus and the rest of Simon's colleagues were eager to fix him up so he'd quit moping around and whining about the horrors of being single.

"More like a client," Simon said.

Marcus resembled a refugee from the sixties, though he wasn't old enough to have experienced the era. He was tall and slender, and wore his brown hair to his shoulders, rimless John Lennon glasses, and Birkenstock sandals year-round. Marcus and his wife, Marianne, lived outside of town on four acres of land off a dirt road. Marianne cared for their four daughters, tended a huge garden, baked and cooked, and edited manuscripts for Oxford University Press. The girls went to county public schools. Marcus commuted to Kenan on a battered motorcycle and brown-bagged his lunch. He was a longtime deacon at the most liberal Baptist church in town, one that withdrew from the Southern Baptist Convention years ago. When Simon first met the couple, he suspected that they affected their lifestyle, but he'd since realized that the two were genuine hippies. He envied their relationship and their children, but not necessarily their lifestyle. They lived too far from a good movie theater with surround sound.

Marcus was also a tenured professor in the history department. He had two doctorates, one in history and one in psychology. His field was the history of science, with a special interest in the conflict between faith and scientific inquiry. He had recently published, to critical acclaim, a book on the recantation of Galileo.

"How're your holidays going?" Simon asked him.

"Good," Marcus said. "Dolly still believes in Santa Claus, and Isobel is willing to pretend for our sakes. So there's lots of shushing and tiptoeing around. It's fun; one of those times you don't want them to grow up."

Simon applied himself to his food. Marcus finished his work in a few keystrokes and snapped his computer shut.

"As an occasional psychologist, I need your opinion on something," Simon said.

"Since when?" Marcus said.

"Just listen, will you? This is important."

"Okay, shoot."

"What do you think of past-life memories?"

"I'm not an expert in that area. I know someone who is, though. She lives in a double-wide just outside Apex. You can't miss the place — it's got a big neon sign that says 'Palms read here' in the window."

"I'm serious."

"You can't be. It's garbage."

"You sure?"

"Of course I'm sure. What's wrong with you? Does it have something to do with the woman I saw leaving your office?"

"Just give it to me in a nutshell, okay?"

"No reputable authority believes that people who remember past lives are recalling actual past incarnations."

"So they're inventing the memories?"

"Not consciously. The consensus is that subjects who remember past lives are emotionally disturbed. They piece together these memories from their own lives, books they've read, movies they've seen, desperately in search of excuses for their neuroses. Frequently they're trying to please some quack therapist who leads them on."

"What if the memories surface under hypnosis?"

"I've told you many times how I feel about hypnosis. I despise it. It's an invitation to fantasize. Patients are so suggestible in a trance you can't trust anything they say. The more troubled they are, the easier they are to hypnotize. Then they're at the mercy of the hypnotist. Why do you ask? Because of your so-called client?"

"Yeah."

"Poor woman."

"I know. A friend referred her to me, and I've got to get out of it gracefully."

"Good luck." Marcus packed his laptop computer into his scarred leather briefcase.

"I hope you're coming to our place for Christmas dinner again this year," he said.

"I'll be there," Simon said. "I must avoid my relations at all cost."

Simon enjoyed a few quiet moments in the lounge after Marcus left. It was a good place to reflect on the past. The library of the college when it was founded almost two hundred years ago, the lounge's walls were still lined with wood bookcases, dark with age, filled with leather-bound books printed on heavy paper. They weren't worth much or they'd be in the rare book room of the main library, but they gave the room an air of antiquity and scholarship. Simon stretched out on the leather sofa. He wished he could get out of his appointment with Helen Williams. Her request made him uncomfortable. But, he reassured himself, it wouldn't take more than a few hours of research to prove that this Annie Evans person never existed. He owed Wade Ferrell that much effort. Resolved to get it over with, he punched Helen Williams' telephone number into his cell phone.

"You don't look much like a history professor," Helen said, ushering him into her hotel room.

"How do history professors look?" he asked.

"Like Arthur Schlesinger."

Simon couldn't help but laugh, and she laughed back. He thought again that she was very attractive.

Simon, who was in his early thirties, had dark brown eyes and curly black hair. He wore jeans, a black polo shirt, and a navy blue blazer with leather patches at the elbows. Simon had inherited the Semitic looks and small size of his petite Jewish mother, Rachel Simon, who left Queens, New York, to work for the public health department in Boone, North Carolina. There she'd met and married Simon's father, James Shaw, a professor of classics at Appalachian State University. Simon was their only child.

"You don't look much like a Southerner, either," she said.

"Born and bred. My father's family has lived in Watauga County for generations. I wouldn't live anywhere but North Carolina. And you?"

"I'm not from around here, as the natives would say, but I got here as fast as I could. My family moved to Wilmington from Ohio when I was a baby," she said. "I love the coast. I teach English as a second language and writing skills to adults at Cape Fear Community College. My townhouse sits right on the sound."

She lifted a pile of library books off the only chair in the room and dumped them on the bed.

"I'm a voracious reader," Helen said. "Which is, according to my parents, most of my problem. When I was little, I used to chatter constantly about a previous life. My parents freaked, as you can imagine. They said my imagination was overstimulated from reading too many books, and that I needed to play outdoors more. I quit talking about Annie when they threatened to confiscate my library card."

"So, who else knows about all this?"

"Just Wade, you, and an assortment of mental health professionals. When I was in college and could get around without my parents knowing, I drove to Raleigh a couple of times to talk to Wade about my persistent past-life memories. God, I hate the way that sounds, like I'm a certified nut. It was such a relief that Wade took me seriously. He referred me to, let's see, two psychiatrists and one psychologist. Therapy and medication got me nowhere. I still had the same memories, same dreams, same everything. I gave up and just tried to live with

Annie. It worked for a while. Wade says the stress of my boyfriend wanting us to get married brought the nightmares back."

"I gather from what you said in my office that you want me to find out if these memories of yours are true," Simon said.

"No, I want you to prove that they aren't true. I don't believe in reincarnation. I want to be rid of this obsession."

"The best approach is for us to assume Annie Evans was a real person, and look for evidence of her life. Do you have any idea when she was born? Where she was born? Whether or not she was married? When she died?"

"Not a clue," she said.

"Annie Evans is a very common name."

"You're telling me we can't find out anything about her?"

"We can find references to dozens of Annie Evanses. I just don't see how we can find out which one is the woman you're looking for, or not looking for, so to speak."

"I was hoping there would be hints in my memories you could use."

"Maybe there are. Are you sure that she lived in Raleigh?"

"Yes."

"How?"

"How do you know you live in Raleigh?"

she said. "You don't walk around thinking consciously about it. You just know it."

"We'll start here, then," Simon said.

"I shouldn't ask you to do this. It's so much work."

"Let's see what you've got," Simon said.

"I've typed up my recollections." She handed him five pages, double-spaced. "It's not much," she said. "Just flashes."

"I'm new at this," Simon said. "What do they feel like, these memories?"

"Just regular memories," she said. "Most of them are, well, quite troubling. Some aren't."

"Tell me," Simon said, recalling his conversation with Marcus. "Did any of these memories emerge during a therapy session, or under hypnosis?"

"No," she said. "I've had them all since I was a child. As I said, I've been to several reputable psychiatrists and psychologists. I did, in desperation, once visit a past-regression therapist where I underwent hypnosis. You know what? I didn't remember anything more! And it was almost impossible for me to go into a trance. I'm not sure I really did. The guy was very disappointed in me."

So much for Marcus' theories. If she was telling Simon the truth, that is.

Helen handed him a loose-leaf notebook stuffed with photocopies.

"These are from the 1908 Sears catalog," she said. "I found it in the library in Wilmington. I can't tell you what it felt like to see the pictures in it. I'm familiar with so many of these items."

Simon flipped through page after page of white lacy blouses with balloon sleeves; long, dark skirts that reached to the ankle; corsets, ornate hats adorned with bird feathers, cast-iron cooking pots, Edwardian jewelry, hideous, heavy furniture upholstered in dark velvets; even eyeglasses, canned food, and that new miracle medicine, aspirin.

Several full pages offered cast-iron kitchen ranges for mail-order sale. At the turn of the century, the range was an essential appliance. Cooking and baking were not its only functions. Using firewood, gas, or coal, it warmed the kitchen on the coldest winter days. It had a boiler that kept water hot around the clock for washing dishes, clothing, and people.

"One of my worst memories is of the day a range like this exploded," Helen said, pointing out one of the smaller models. "One morning, I, or Annie Evans that is, was feeding chickens in the backyard of a frame house, out in the country somewhere. It was a very cold day — I was wearing a heavy shawl and could see my breath in the air. The stove exploded and I ran to the back door of the house, into the kitchen full of flames. The floor was covered with bits of metal and scraps of burning wood. I dragged a dead man, horribly burned, out of the kitchen and into the backyard. The house burned to the ground while I screamed. No one heard me and no one came to help me. That's all I remember."

"Do you know who the man was?"

"Not for sure. I've always assumed he was my husband."

Suddenly, the absurdity of their conversation struck Simon. What was he doing? No matter how normal this woman seemed, she had more problems than he could solve. He'd do this favor for Wade as quickly as possible, keep quiet about it, and then wash his hands of the situation. If word got out that he was researching someone's so-called past life, it could trash his academic reputation.

"Let me take these papers home with me," he said. "And I'll get back to you."

He could tell from her expression that she was disappointed by his abruptness, but she politely showed him to the door. She didn't ask him how long it would be until he called her, or what he thought. She just shook his hand, almost as if it wouldn't surprise her if she didn't hear from him again.

Simon parked his Thunderbird in his carport and covered it. He'd gotten lucky — he couldn't afford one of the new 2002 models when they were first available, but then found one that had been repossessed after being driven less than ten thousand miles. His car was the evening black version with a tan interior. The winter had been mild so far, so he hadn't changed over the white softop for the black hardtop. He could still drive with the top down on a sunny afternoon. Simon loved the retro look of the car, especially the inset headlights and portholes. His earlier model Thunderbird was now parked next door. His neighbor's teenage son, Danny, was working off what he was paying for it by playing keyboards at holiday parties around town.

As Simon walked onto his porch, dusk reached just the right intensity to trigger the Christmas lights strung in the trees on his block. As if on cue, the lights flashed on in unison. Simon paused to enjoy the sight. He decided that he preferred fat colored lights to tiny white ones, but he was open to changing his mind tomorrow.

All evening, Simon ignored the thin sheaf of papers that Helen Williams had given him. Instead of reading them, he piddled around his Craftsman-style bungalow doing whatever chores he could think of, feeding his cats, sorting the mail, loading the dishwasher, and watching the evening news. Then he dined on the rich leftovers his next-door neighbor had brought him after her party last weekend — beef tenderloin, tiny buttery rolls, grape tomato and tortellini kabobs, toasted pecans. The food was partly penance — it was an office party and he hadn't been invited.

Simon didn't often allow himself to dwell on the unsatisfactory aspects of his life. He'd been so lucky in many respects: His aunts and uncles and cousins adored him, he had good friends, and he had a successful career. He'd adjusted to being an orphan. But he wasn't ashamed to admit that he wished he was married. He wasn't impressed by the so-called freedoms of the single life. He was divorced from his first and only wife and had just broken up with his girlfriend, police attorney Julia McGloughlin, mostly because he was serious and she wasn't. He'd dumped her preemptively, in other words. He'd been frustrated in love often enough to begin to wonder if he'd find himself in exactly the same situation, a bachelor at Christmas, ten years from now.

There was a little tenderloin left over from his dinner. Simon cut it into bits and summoned his cats. Maybelline, who couldn't be true, was the *mater familias*. Her daughters were Ruby, who took her love to town, and Cecilia, who broke hearts. He had finally done the responsible thing and had all three of them spayed. Now they beat up all the local tomcats instead of luring them into his backyard, caterwauling with passion.

The images of the kitchen fire Helen had described to him earlier had wandered in and out of his mind all evening, and he thought of them again as he flicked on the gas fire in his fireplace. He couldn't ignore her packet of memories any longer.

Annie's Memories

It's wintertime and deep snow covers the ground up to the fender of the one automobile, a Packard, I think, parked in front of the largest brick building on the property where I live. I think that the facility must be a school — there are a number of institutional brick buildings arranged in a semi-

circle within a beautiful wooded property, thick with tall oaks. There are children and teachers living in most of the houses. One building is a kitchen and dining hall, and another is a hospital. I live in the smallest building within the semicircle. Despite its acreage, the school's not in the country because outside the fence to the south are streets lined with homes and businesses.

I walk out of a gate, across a packed-earth alley, and down a side street. I've made this trip many times before. I'm on my way to visit someone important to me and I don't want to miss it, in spite of the weather. It's dusk, and I'm wrapped in a heavy coat and wearing a wide black felt hat decorated with raven's wings. No one else is out and about. The trolley tracks are covered in snow, and the wires sag under its weight. I pass by a grocery store, locked up tight, but the window is stacked with a pyramid of canned goods, which I stop to admire. I was disappointed. I'd planned to buy a box of chocolates to take with me. On my walk, I pass by a dozen bungalows, their Victorian parlors lit by oil lamps. In front of one house, a horse is tied to a painted iron stableboy holding a lantern and a ring. The horse wears a rough blanket and stomps to keep himself warm, blowing air from his nostrils. For some reason, I am sure that it's near Christmas, 1910.

The next passage repeated the story Helen had told him earlier that afternoon.

In the memory which I think is the earliest chronologically, I'm a young woman feeding the chickens outside a farmhouse. I'm wearing a knit shawl and heavy boots caked with mud. As I scatter corn, I talk to the hens and baby chicks at my feet like you would talk to a pet or a young child, silly words that don't mean anything. It's early morning, the sun is just rising, and I think that it's going to be a pretty day.

Suddenly, there's a terrible explosion. Terrified, I drop the bucket of food; the chickens scatter everywhere. Looking back at the house, I see that the kitchen is full of flames. I run toward it and into the kitchen, where the range has exploded, raining hot metal and boiling water. A man lies on the floor, black with burns and coal dust. I drag him outside, where I watch the house burn to the ground. There's nothing I can do. There's no telephone, no way to summon help. I kneel beside the dead man, holding his hand and crying.

★ ★ ★

I'm sitting at a window, sewing, with a basket of mending at my feet. The basket is full of white linen undergarments, in all sizes. Most have been mended at least once already. Outside the window, dogwood, apple, and cherry trees bloom in the vast green grounds of the school. There are two teenage girls helping me. We're wearing long plain cotton dresses and full-length aprons. As I gaze out the window, I notice a column of barefoot boys processing solemnly across the lawn. The littlest ones are crying hard. The teenage boy leading the group carries something tiny cradled in both hands. Another, head bent reverently, holds a Bible close to his chest. I'm angry — I throw down the mending and rush outside — the big boys scatter, and I comfort the little ones, wiping their tears away with the hem of my apron.

This is my recurring nightmare; it never varies:

It's deeply dark, except for a small pool of light thrown by a lantern resting on the ground. It's snowing hard and I'm digging a hole next to a large gravestone. The stone is engraved, but I can't read the inscription. The ground is frozen, but I'm strong and I keep digging. There's a bundle wrapped in clothing at my feet. When I've finished digging the hole, I pick up the bundle. I move away some of the cloths, and I see the face of a dead baby about eighteen months old. It's dressed in a lacy outfit and cap, and has curly blond hair and a tiny chin dimple. I can't see its eyes because they're closed, but somehow I know that they're blue, and I know that the child is a girl. I kiss the baby on the forehead, then bury it in the hole, covering it with dirt, spreading sticks and damp leaves on top, then covering the spot with snow. I kneel next to the grave and pray.

It's Christmas Day, some years later, I think. One of the school buildings is crowded with children and teachers. The children are dressed in their best clothes — the boys in knickers and white shirts, the girls in dark skirts, black hose, and middy blouses. I'm dressed up, too, in a black and white checked floor-length ruffled skirt and a white blouse with puffed sleeves, tucked with lace. I'm wearing a silver locket, spectacles that hang from a silver chain, and a brooch watch pinned with the face upside down so I can read it. My hair is dressed like a Gibson girl's, in a puffed-up knot secured with a tortoiseshell comb. We — the adults and children — are having a wonderful dinner of turkey, ham, mashed potatoes, carrots, peas, and yeast rolls with fresh butter. Apple and pecan pies wait for us on a sideboard. Then we crowd into a drawing room with a twelve-foot-tall Christmas tree decorated with garlands of popcorn and real candles. There's a bucket of water nearby in case the tree catches fire! A man dressed as Santa Claus calls out names and gives each child two gifts. They react with glee, as if they've gotten a fortune's worth of toys. Most of the boys get candy, flashlights, or comic books, while the girls receive hair ribbons, tiny Kewpie dolls, or sewing kits. Several of the girls present me with handmade presents — one is a handkerchief embroidered with my initials, and I recall feeling especially pleased. The little girl who gives it to me is about eight years old, with blond curly hair; she wears a navy middy blouse with a red tie.

As the children leave the building, each gets an orange and a small bag of nuts handed to them at the door by a white-haired man who's dressed like those pictures you see of Teddy Roosevelt, complete with knickers and a monocle.

2

> I shall not commit the fashionable stupidity of regarding everything I cannot explain as a fraud.
>
> — CARL JUNG

Simon tossed Helen Williams' memories on the coffee table, stretched, and massaged his temples. Then he rolled his head across the back of the sofa, trying to work out the tension in his neck that had accumulated as he read. He didn't know who he was more embarrassed for, the woman who wrote this drivel, or himself, for reading it. The pages read like excerpts from a bad Gothic novel. He couldn't believe that he was expected to take it seriously.

He went into his kitchen, got a cold Coke out of the refrigerator, popped the top, and stirred in two Goody's Powders, his personal headache remedy. Sometimes it worked. He drank it down.

He wondered what on earth to do next. He briefly considered never contacting Helen Williams again, but he couldn't do that and face Wade Ferrell. He'd have to produce something, some kind of research, to put Williams off and satisfy his obligation to Wade. And to placate his own conscience, for that matter. He'd promised both of them that he'd help, and he took giving his word seriously. How did one go about researching a figment of someone's imagination? The only way he could think of was to assume Annie Evans did exist and try to find evidence of her life. When he couldn't produce any proof that she'd lived, surely his job would be done.

Simon went upstairs to the small third bedroom that served as his home study, sat down at his desk, and hit the play button on his CD player. He'd rediscovered Appalachian music on a recent visit to Boone, and had brought home a couple of CDs of the classics. As an a cappella harmony of "Down to the River to Pray" filled the room, he turned on his laptop computer, logged onto the Internet, and signed into a popular genealogy Web site. He entered "Annie Evans" into the search engine. He got 2,775 hits, all useless since it was impossible to know which entry was the correct Annie Evans. He needed a fact — like her birthday or the date of her death — to narrow down his search, assuming that the woman he was searching for was a real person, which she certainly wasn't. What a waste of his time. He printed out the list of hits to show to Helen Williams tomorrow.

Simon had accomplished all he could for now. He'd also need to spend a few hours at the library in order to satisfy himself that he'd done enough to discharge his obligation.

First thing the next morning, Simon stopped by the history department office to see if anyone had brought in food. He'd finished the party leftovers in his refrigerator, two ham puffs and three cold shrimp, for breakfast.

"Sorry," said Judy Smith, the departmental secretary. "No food today. Thank God. I've already gained two pounds."

Judy was collating exams at her desk, stacking and stapling deftly despite her long, polished fingernails. She was still the country girl who first came to work at the department several years ago, looking for a second husband in the big city. She dyed her hair red (Autumn Mist), chewed gum constantly, kept a cold bottle of Sundrop on her desk at all times, and took her lunch hour at a time when she could watch her favorite soap opera. She was still pursuing

Mr. Right. The current candidate was a fireman based at the fire station on the corner of Park Drive and Oberlin Road.

"Don't forget to check your box," Judy said.

Since the e-mail era began, the faculty seldom used the neatly labeled wooden cubbyholes that lined a wall of the office. Today, though, a folded paper protruded from Simon's box.

"It's from one of your fans," Judy said, "she was here bright and early this morning.

"What are you talking about?"

"The note from a student who wants to get into your historiography seminar next semester."

"Preregistration is over. The class is full."

"That won't stop them. Do you know how good that seminar will look on a student's transcript? It's not every undergraduate who can take a class taught by a celebrity professor such as yourself."

"I hate that expression, Judy, you know that. And the only way someone else can get in the class is if a preregistered student doesn't show up."

"You'd better have a plan to deal with it."

Simon stuck the note in his pocket and went to the faculty lounge. Thank God no one was there, and that the coffee was ready. There was no food in sight, but it was early yet. He filled his mug, ladled in milk and sugar, and went to his office, where he read the note before beginning his work.

The note was scribbled on a piece of paper torn from an exam blue book. *"Dear Dr. Shaw,"* he read. *"You don't know me, but I sure have heard of you. I've read your book, and I really enjoyed it. I mean, I haven't finished it yet, but I will over break. This college is so lucky to have someone like you teaching here! By the way, I didn't preregister for your class. I think that if there are any vacancies, they should be filled on a first-come, first-serve basis. I got here at six thirty this morning! I had to get security to open the door! Sincerely, Mary-Fish Cameron."*

Mary-Fish had drawn an adorable smiley face next to her signature. Simon winced. The bottom third of Kenan College's student body was composed of average students whose parents could afford to pay full tuition. Just because they weren't National Merit Scholars didn't mean they didn't deserve good teaching, but honest to God, sometimes he didn't know why some of them bothered. Postponing getting a job, he supposed. He balled up the note and lobbed it into the trash can. Then he thought better of it; he didn't know what college rules applied here. He'd better keep track of Miss Cameron's name in case he had openings in the seminar. Surely there wouldn't be a scene when the first class met. He hoped some of the students registered in order to learn something, instead of because he'd gotten his picture in People. The balled-up note was damp with spilled coffee, but he dredged it out of his trash can, spread it flat, and put it in a file folder, with the date and time scribbled on it. If he had any future openings in his seminar, he wanted no controversy over who had contacted him first.

Simon put the spectacle of a mob of rioting students beating on the door of Seminar Room 203 out of his mind and turned to his computer. He was finishing up a brain-busting exam for North Carolina History. This year he thought he'd challenge his students with one hundred and fifty short-answer questions. It wasn't like he hadn't warned them. When the usual half-dozen students asked him what they needed to study for the exam, he had answered each one of them the same way: "Everything."

A message intruded on his computer screen, indicating he had e-mail. As he opened his mailbox, "Urgent!" in bright orange letters flashed in the message's subject line. The missive came by way of the campus server, so he felt obliged to read it.

"Dear Professor Shaw," it began. *"Thank you so much for offering your seminar, The Writing of History, again this year. It will undoubtedly be the best course available in the college next semester, especially since class size is limited to fifteen. Unfortunately, I failed to preregister. I was busy tutoring underprivileged children at Wiley Elementary School at the time. Did you know that according to university policy you can deny admission to up to three preregistered students if a more qualified student applies later? You should know that I'm double-majoring in History and English. I had an article entitled 'Hemingway's Literary Journalism' published last year in the* Columbia Journalism Review, *and I'm a Kenan Scholar (3.91 GPA). I'll be waiting outside class on the first day of the seminar. I'll wear my varsity golf jacket so you'll recognize me. Best Wishes, Jay Harris Kennedy (no relation)."*

With a heavy heart, Simon printed out Kennedy's e-mail, wrote the date and time on it, and stuck it in the file folder with Miss Cameron's note. Something told him this wouldn't be the last request he got.

Simon finished writing the exam, burned the original file to a CD, printed out a master copy, and deleted the file on his hard drive so some campus geek couldn't hack into his computer and steal it. Then he locked the exam in a lockbox in the back of a file cabinet. He'd print the required number of copies himself half an hour before the exam. Many professors were fatalistic about cheating, but Simon considered foiling it part of his job.

Ready for another infusion of caffeine and a serious snack, Simon went downstairs to the faculty lounge. Marcus and Jack were there, grading term papers at one of the library tables. Unfortunately, so was Vera, who perched on the leather sofa with her open briefcase on the coffee table in front of her, reading a term paper, too. There was no food available, and the fresh pot of coffee wasn't ready. Simon could hardly turn around and leave, so he sat down near Vera to wait for the coffee to brew.

"I'm glad you came in, Simon," Vera said, snapping her briefcase shut. "I want to talk to you about something."

Professor Vera Thayer was a short, stubby woman who dressed meticulously in a suit every day, wore full makeup, and had her iron gray hair twisted into a French knot twice a week. She'd risen in Kenan's academic ranks in a time when faculty women didn't get maternity leave unless they delivered in the summer, and were expected to be able to type and take shorthand so they could keep the minutes at faculty meetings. Whatever her faults, she was tough as an old boot.

"Of course, Vera," Simon said.

"One of my best students, Jay Kennedy, missed preregistration for your writing seminar next semester. I'd appreciate it if you'd admit him."

Behind Vera, at the library table, Jack and Marcus stopped grading papers and settled back to watch the fireworks.

"I can't do that," Simon said. "The class is full."

"Of course you can," Vera said. "You can replace any student with a better qualified one."

"I'm not going to do that," Simon said. "It's a bad policy. Besides, another student's already asked. I've started a waiting list. Kennedy's name is second on it."

"That's ridiculous. No one's going to drop out, short of two broken legs. For once, think about the department's reputation. Jay's got a shot at Yale graduate school. We must get some of our students into Ivy League programs to stay competitive. And Jay's a Kenan Scholar, you know."

"I'd rather have one student in the seminar who's gone to the trouble to preregister for it than a dozen Jay Kennedys," Simon said. "I don't care how many academic scalps they've collected. Sorry, Jack."

An amused Jack Kingfisher waved off Simon's politically incorrect remark. "No offense taken," he said.

When the bell for the next class rang, Jack and Vera got up to leave, but Vera couldn't resist a parting shot.

"If you won't admit Jay to your class, Simon, I'm afraid I'll have to speak to Walker about it."

"Go right ahead," Simon said. He and Vera had clashed over Vera's pet students before. Walker Jones would never interfere with Simon's right to run his classes the way he saw fit.

Both Vera and Jack left the lounge, Jack holding the door open for her as she stalked out.

"Was the cup of coffee worth it?" Marcus asked.

"Just barely," Simon said, pouring a mug and adding milk and sugar.

"Look," Marcus said. "I've got to come back tonight to grade papers after I do some Christmas shopping. Want to have dinner?"

"Sure. Where do you want to go?"

"Make it the cafeteria," Marcus said. "I'm on a tight schedule."

"Me, too." Simon wanted to get to the library and then meet with Helen Williams before the end of the day.

"It's not easy to shop for my girls anymore," Marcus said. "Used to be, I could go to that monster toy store and get everything they wanted. Now I've got to hit half the stores in the mall. I draw the line at clothes. Marianne has to cope with that. They all want tops that show their navels. I can't bear it."

They agreed to meet at six thirty at the cafeteria, and Simon went back to his office. He stared at his telephone for a while before he had the nerve to call Helen Williams and set up a time to meet that afternoon. He couldn't wait to get this monkey off his back. Make it five o'clock, he thought. He'd plead his dinner engagement with Marcus to get out of spending much time with her.

"Hi there," Simon said to her, after she'd answered the phone in her hotel room.

"Hi," she said back. "You can't be done already."

"Let's just say I have a progress report," he said. "Can I come by about five?"

"Certainly. My social calendar isn't exactly booked up," she said.

Simon was struck again by how normal she sounded. But she had to be disturbed, didn't she? Why else would she believe she remembered living almost a hundred years ago?

Every chair in the Kenan College library was occupied by disheveled, bleary-eyed students who'd stayed up all night studying. With bags under their eyes, soft-drink cans and candy wrappers stuffed into gaping backpacks, they bent over notes and textbooks. Several were asleep. Simon didn't feel sorry for them. He expected his students to work hard. He'd done the same in his day. He still worked long hours grading papers and exams late into the night, sitting through endless curriculum meetings, reworking lectures to reflect new historical knowledge, and designing seminars that would challenge his students and himself, instead of relying on whatever he'd done the previous year.

Simon unlocked his carrel, dropped his briefcase onto the chair, and checked his desk to see if the librarians had absconded with any of the books he'd reserved. Good. *Roanoke Island* by Ann Miller and *Operation Drumbeat* by Michael Gammon were still there, with sticky notes marking the pages mentioning primary sources he wanted to consult for his proposed book on the coastal history of North Carolina.

Simon left his carrel and went down a flight of steps to the basement microfilm reading room. More students were there feverishly researching term papers that should have been written days ago.

Simon found the spool of microfilm for the *Raleigh News and Observer* for the month of December 1910, since Helen "remembered" Christmas of that year.

Simon loved reading old newspapers. The hypnotic whirring of the microfilm machines, the archaic language of articles and advertisements, and the grainy monochromatic pictures worked on his consciousness almost like a time machine. He felt transported into the past and lost all track of time. He paged through the microfilm, not taking notes, just soaking up atmosphere, but staying alert for an item that might verify Helen's story.

Simon thought that, somehow, the turn of the century in America felt more remote than just a hundred years ago. Everyday life seemed so primitive then. Cities in most regions of the country looked like the frontier towns in old Western movies — one dusty street lined with clapboard buildings and wooden sidewalks. Single dirt roads left the towns and petered out in open fields. Almost everyone earned their living in agriculture. People lived in shacks and log cabins and adobes and sod cabins, owned two changes of clothes, went barefoot except in the dead of winter, and worked from dawn to dusk, six days a week. Only along the eastern seaboard did life hint at the coming of the modern age.

It had snowed in Raleigh that December. A front-page photograph looked down Raleigh's main street toward the stone capitol building. Snow drifted up to the running boards of the two automobiles parked along the empty street. Canvas awnings jutted from stolid brick Edwardian office buildings to cover wooden sidewalks. Electric light bulbs outlined a sign that read "Drugs" mounted on one building. Other than aspirin, which had just been invented by Bayer, the pharmacist who worked there could offer his customers little more than cod liver oil, laudanum, Carter's liver pills, and Miss Pinkham's Female Tonic. Coca-Cola, originally invented as a headache remedy, relied on cocaine for its refreshing properties. Whiskey was taken medicinally when all other relief failed. Though North

Carolina had ratified a state prohibition law in 1908, liquor was still available at pharmacies with a doctor's prescription.

Another photograph of Raleigh, taken on a clear day, showed a wide cobbled boulevard several blocks long that divided downtown. Horses and buggies and a few automobiles hugged the curbs. The middle of the street was reserved for the trolley cars and their tracks, powered by overhead electric lines, their bells clanging soundlessly across the decades. Telegraph poles lined the sidewalk. There were few telephones yet. Most people communicated by wire, even across town. Men hurried to work wearing bowler hats and carrying walking sticks. Women wore dark dresses down to their ankles and lavish hats, and carried shopping bags as they strolled down the street.

Single people, both men and women, lived in hotels or boarding houses. "Spinsters" kept house for their male relatives or lived on meager allowances. Men worked sixty hours a week at trades or small business. Few women had marketable job skills. Widowed women with children were often desperate and destitute. The invention of the typewriter opened up a new, respectable way for women to earn a living. "Girl typists" were independent, desirable, and could take their time choosing a husband. Ironically, years later, the typewriter became a symbol of female servitude.

Ads for canned goods and a new product, Kellogg's Corn Flakes, reminded Simon that cooking a hot meal in those days required hours of preparation — toting wood or coal for the stove, sweating over its uneven heat, and finally washing the dishes by hand with water from the range's broiler. Oysters, Marmite, turtle soup, chipped beef, sweetbreads, and a new dessert, brownies, were the fashionable foods of the era.

Men chewed, smoked, and spat tobacco, and whiled evenings away playing cards in clubs. Nickelodeons projected primitive one-reel dramas, comedies, and Westerns. Most entertainment was live — the piano and fiddle in the parlor, the circus, a musical review, the state fair. Businessmen watched the prices of cotton, tobacco, sugar, and wool rise and fall, and complained about the greed of Standard Oil and the sugar trust. The celebrities of the day were the fabulously rich. Gossip columns and society pages slobbered over their romances, parties, and spending sprees.

Racial attitudes were such that an editorial writer could actually describe that "happy day when darkies all were happy and slavery made them faithful, kind, and the best of companions." Most adults alive remembered the Civil War. There was an old Confederate soldiers' home in Raleigh, and the town turned out for a massive celebration every January 19 in honor of Robert E. Lee's birthday.

The reference to Lee's birthday briefly reminded Simon of the present. North Carolina still flew the Confederate flag, the "Stars and Bars," over the state capitol on Lee's birthday. The practice, hinting as it did of slavery and the horrors of the Civil War, enraged him. He couldn't drive past the capitol building without feeling his blood pressure surge. Simon's annual blast at the practice had become a fixture on the editorial page of the *News and Observer*. For about a month, each year after his article appeared, he'd lock his doors day and night, shut off his voice mail, delete his e-mail messages without reading them, and keep his baseball bat under his bed in case some misguided son of the Old South tried to hurt him.

He'd started writing this year's broadside in his head and would polish it to perfection after Christmas. This year, he planned a new attack — using Lee's own words. Simon remembered that Lee once said something like "let's furl the flag," which would be such an apt phrase for his editorial. For once, his photographic memory failed him, and for the life of him he couldn't remember the source. He'd hired one of his students, for ten dollars an hour, to look for the reference over Christmas break. If she couldn't find it, he'd have to fall back on "let's strike the tent," Lee's last words.

Simon pulled his focus back to the turn of the century, and resumed his reading.

In 1910, Christmas advertisements in the newspaper touted books as Christmas presents. For children, booksellers suggested *The Emerald City of Oz* by Frank Baum, a half-dozen Tom Swift titles for boys, and *Rebecca of Sunnybrook Farm* for girls. E. M. Forster's latest, *Howard's End*, was an adult best-seller.

William Howard Taft, the oversized former Secretary of War, had succeeded the legendary Theodore Roosevelt as President of the United States. A feature article made much of Taft's Christmas shopping. He bought hundreds of gifts for friends, relatives, and employees, a task that took three solid days of shopping, mostly rummaging the shelves of various booksellers, since he preferred to give books. In this, he was a man after Simon's own heart.

On December 21, John D. Rockefeller gave ten million dollars to the University of Chicago, the last installment of an astounding thirty-five-million-dollar gift.

On Christmas Eve, the State Department sent a check for five thousand dollars to China for famine relief.

Sunday morning, Christmas Day, was quiet since every decent person in Raleigh was in church. In the afternoon, parades and fireworks filled the streets.

Simon shut off the microfilm reader. Helen's memories had a genuine turn-of-the-century atmosphere, but she could have researched the period herself, in any library in North Carolina.

Before he left the building, Simon consulted the 1910 Raleigh City Directory. No Annie Evans was listed there.

Helen answered the door a second after Simon knocked.

"I forgot to give you something," she said. Eagerly she thrust a sheet of paper into his hand.

"It's a map I've drawn. It's a plan of the place where Annie lived," she said.

Helen's map was a sketch of a semicircular group of about a dozen squares representing buildings carefully labeled in capital letters. A road curved around the buildings. A large square in the center of the grouping was labeled "main building?," a smaller one outside the circle was marked "hospital?," and another small building read "Annie's home?" On the outskirts of the complex, a large area had been labeled "farm or barn?"

Simon looked up at Helen.

"This is it?" he said.

"Isn't it helpful?" she asked.

"Well," Simon said, "I don't know what it is, where it is, or anything."

"It's a campus," she said. "A school. Something like that."

Simon didn't answer. The last thing he needed was a new lead. He wanted to get this pathetic business over with.

"I'm afraid I haven't accomplished much," Simon said. He sat down on the desk chair while she sat on the bed. "You see, it's virtually impossible to trace an ordinary person born before World War I. There are almost no records. States weren't required to document births or deaths. Social Security records didn't exist before 1933."

"Oh," she said.

"Women are especially difficult," Simon said, "because they changed their names with marriage. Property and tax information was recorded in the name of male heads of household — husbands, fathers, or sons."

"I see," she said. "What about church archives?"

"Churches kept baptism, burial, and marriage records, but we'd have to know where Annie attended church."

"In other words, we'd have to already know most of the answers to my questions."

"I'm afraid so."

Simon was relieved that she understood the situation clearly.

"So what do we do now?" she asked.

"I've done all I can," he said.

If Simon could have predicted her reaction, he would never have been so curt. She transformed in front of his eyes from an eager, hopeful, and attractive woman into a disappointed and depressed human being. Her smile vanished, her shoulders slumped, and she started to turn and twist the hem of her sweater into a knot.

"You can't help me any further?" she asked.

"I'm sorry, I . . ."

"It's all right, I understand," she said. "I shouldn't have presumed, I mean I know you just did this much for Wade, but I'd hoped for more information."

"I wish I could do more," Simon said. He didn't wish anything of the kind, and he felt like a cad for abandoning her.

"Thank you for your help," she said, rising and extending her hand to him.

Simon shook her hand.

"What will you do now?" he said.

"I don't know," she said. "But it's not your problem anymore."

3

I am confident that there is truly such a thing as living again. That the living spring from the dead and the souls of the dead are in existence.

— SOCRATES

"It's not your problem anymore." Helen Williams' last words to him lingered uncomfortably in Simon's mind as he waited in the lobby of the Kenan College cafeteria for Marcus. Helen had seemed crushed when he told her he was through with his research. He wondered if he could have done more to help her. As soon as that fleeting thought came to him, he repressed it. He'd talk to Marcus about it at dinner. His friend would urge him to stay far away from Helen Williams and her problems.

Simon unloaded his tray at a table for two in the faculty dining room.

"Not feeling sociable?" Marcus asked, sitting down opposite him, glancing around the room at the larger tables full of chatting faculty.

"No, I'm not. Besides, I want to talk to you privately," Simon said.

For a few minutes, the two men concentrated on their bowls of homemade Brunswick stew, thick with chicken, pork, and vegetables, and their cracklin' corn bread, both specialties of the Kenan College cafeteria.

When they had finished eating, Simon fetched mugs of hot coffee for both of them.

"This private matter you want to talk about, it's not about your lousy love life, is it?" Marcus asked. "You've exhausted all of Marianne's single friends. Have you considered the personals?"

"I tried writing an ad once, but I got bored with myself before I finished. That's not what I wanted to talk to you about."

"What then?"

"Past-life memories."

Marcus groaned. "What's gotten into you?" he said. "It's that so-called client of yours, that woman — am I right? She's good-looking, I admit, but if you get involved with her and her fantasies, it could ruin your career."

"I promised to help her. I've done a bad job so far because her problem makes me uncomfortable."

"Drop it. I guarantee you that Helen Williams didn't live in the past. She's an emotionally disturbed person. Mind you, she's not alone. If all the pathetic sods who insist they were present at the Crucifixion really were, there wouldn't have been room on Calvary for the two thieves."

"Helen doesn't claim anything so wild. And she seems to me to have plenty of self-esteem. If anything, worrying that she had a past incarnation is ruining her life, not enhancing it."

"Most of these poor souls believe that they were not just one famous person, but dozens — Michelangelo, and Charlemagne, and Pope Paul."

"She's not claiming to be anyone famous, either."

"That's something. Are you going to eat all your pie?"

Simon shoved the remaining half of his pecan pie across the table.

"Want some more coffee?" Simon asked.

"Sure."

"The price is a serious discussion."

"If you insist, I'll try."

Simon refilled their mugs of coffee and brought them back to the table.

"Let me illustrate what I'm trying to say with the most famous 'reincarnation' case of all, Bridey Murphy," Marcus said. "She was the nineteenth-century Irish woman who emerged whenever a Denver housewife named Virginia Tighe was hypnotized by candlelight back in the 1950s."

"Her hypnotist wrote a famous book, right?"

"That's the one. But a reporter from the local paper took Mrs. Tighe's story to pieces with very little effort. Bridey Murphy supposedly lived in Ireland in 1806, and under hypnosis Tighe remembered all kinds of unique and vivid details of the times. But it turned out that Tighe had once lived with an aunt of Irish descent who often regaled her niece with stories about the old country. And later, another reporter investigating Tighe's claims discovered that a woman named Bridie Murphy Corkell had lived across the street from Tighe in Chicago. Tighe didn't deliberately mislead anyone. She had a classic case of cryptoamnesia. You see, the human mind overflows with years and years worth of overheard conversations, pictures, newspaper stories, books, television shows, movies, and songs. Nothing is ever lost — these bits and pieces of information and experience form the basis of fully blown fantasies that emerge, under hypnosis, as personal 'memories.' "

"Past-life regression, that's what they call

it, right? If it's such a disreputable notion, how did it get started?"

"Freud taught us to return to early childhood for the source of our neuroses. Then Otto Rank got the bright idea to lead patients even further back to past lives and death experiences, traumas that survive as 'memories of the soul' that cause various afflictions in the present. It works like this: A man with persistent neck pain 'remembers' being guillotined in eighteenth-century France, and, boom, his neck pain disappears!"

"I assume you think it's bunk."

"It's pseudoscience, and that's the best you can say about it. Other terms that come to mind are charlatanism and quackery. We all have one life. If you have a pain in your neck, it may be due to hunching over your computer screen, or your wife hassling you, or maybe a touch of arthritis. The solutions to most people's emotional problems are behavioral. Change your job, divorce your wife, whatever. Therapy that concentrates on blame instead of coping has turned our culture into a refuge for whiners."

"Buddhists and Hindus believe in reincarnation. That's millions of people."

"Lots of Christians believe that the theory of evolution is a satanic deception. That doesn't make them right."

Simon had finished his coffee. He'd been alternately scribbling notes from Marcus' conversation on a napkin and doodling tornadoes whirling around its edges.

"You don't seem convinced," Marcus said.

"I agree with every word you've said. I just can't square any of it with Helen Williams."

"Okay," Marcus said. "Let me do one thing for you before you go poking around in the vast library of paranormal phenomena. Of the hundreds of books and articles written on paranormal subjects, there are a few that are reputable."

Simon looked at him sharply.

"You just told me it was all bullshit."

Marcus shrugged. "There has been some scientific work on psychic phenomena."

"I'm astounded you'd admit such a thing."

"If there is such a thing as ESP, or precognition, there's a rational, physical mechanism for it, not a paranormal or supernatural one."

"I often know who's on the other end of the phone when it rings."

"Those are random incidents. We've all had them. You just don't remember all the times the phone rings and you were wrong about who was calling. But back to reincarnation. There are a few case studies of past-life recollections that are compelling, mostly of children. We can't explain them yet."

"I'd like to see them."

"Let me put together some notes for you."

"Thanks. I appreciate it."

"Listen," Marcus said, leaning across the table. "Just satisfy your intellectual curiosity, okay? Stay away from that Williams woman. Just because you have tenure doesn't mean they can't move your office to a broom closet."

A box with the familiar return address of his Uncle Morris Simon's deli on Pearl Street in New York City waited on Simon's porch. Simon started salivating before he even got his front door unlocked. He tore open the box in his kitchen, revealing fresh-baked bagels dusted with kosher salt, his uncle's own recipe for herbed cream cheese packed in dry ice, and his aunt's rugulach — mini-strudel with a flaky cream cheese crust, bursting with raisins, nuts, and cinnamon, carefully packed in a crushproof container. He stuffed himself with the rugulach, saving the bagels for breakfast in the morning.

Hanukkah candles lay at the bottom of the gift box wrapped in a blue and white ribbon stamped with a Star of David, meant for Simon's mother's menorah. Simon found the sterling silver menorah in his sideboard, placed the candles in it, and set it on his fireplace mantel. He had no clue what day in the Hanukkah holiday it was, so he lit all the candles. The effect was quite nice, with the gleaming menorah nestled among the swathe of Fraser fir that his aunt had sent him from the family Christmas tree farm in Boone.

One day, he was going to have to make a decision about the religion thing. In his heart, he suspected he'd choose Judaism. There were already plenty of Baptists in his family, and a paucity of observant Jews. He'd have to wait until his Aunt Rae Coffey, who'd been the first female Elder in her little country Baptist church, either died or was living on an Alzheimer's ward somewhere. She believed that everyone in the world who wasn't a primitive Baptist was going to hell. It would break her heart to have to give up on Simon's salvation.

Simon spent the rest of the evening sipping a bourbon in his living room and planning the next few days. It was Wednesday night. He'd graded all his term papers and finished composing his exams. The next two days, Thursday and Friday, were college reading days. He'd keep his office hours in case his students needed him. He had a neighbor's book club meeting to attend. Otherwise, he intended to finish his Christmas shopping. He just had to make three stops — the bookstore, the music store, and the wine shop. Nobody on his list needed anything else. Over the weekend, he'd attend Sergeant Otis Gates' and his wife Alma's famous open house, which he didn't intend to miss even if Julia, his former girlfriend, was there. He also wanted to connect with his close friend David Morgan, an archeologist with the North Carolina Department of Archaeology, before Morgan left for Tennessee to spend the holiday with his sister and her family.

Simon wondered if Helen Williams would go back to Wilmington now, and if he should call Wade Ferrell and report what he had accomplished. He was embarrassed that he'd done so little, so he decided to read Marcus' notes on reincarnation studies before talking to Wade.

As he undressed for bed, Simon found Helen's map folded up in his jacket pocket.

He turned it around in his hands a few times, studying it, then was struck with a twinge of familiarity that kept him looking at it for a long time before he turned off his light.

Late the next morning, Simon was driving down St. Mary's Street with his passenger seat full of presents when he spotted Helen Williams walking along the sidewalk. She was several blocks from her hotel, probably just out for exercise, but when he got closer to her he was concerned. She didn't look well. She walked slowly, dragging her feet, with her shoulders hunched and her gaze fixed on the ground. None of my business, Simon thought. Then Helen stopped and stared into the heavy traffic zooming by. She stepped off the curb. Simon turned sharply into the Broughton High School parking lot, screeched around it in a tight circle, and pulled out into the street again, stopping crookedly in the parking space in front of her. She lifted her eyes and registered surprise when she recognized him. He lowered his car window to speak to her.

"Are you all right?" he asked.

"Of course," she said. "I've been waiting for a break in this traffic so I can cross the street, that's all." Up close, she still didn't look well. She had deep circles under her eyes and her face and lips were pale. Her hands were stuffed into the pockets of her red Christmas sweater. He resisted the urge to point out to her that the sweater was buttoned crookedly.

"It's none of my business . . . ," he began.

"No, it's not," she said. "I'll think I'll finish my walk in the park over there," she said, nodding her head toward the still green acres that stretched behind the row of buildings on St. Mary's Street.

"Good-bye, Professor Shaw," she said. "Have a nice day."

She turned and walked off.

Simon slapped the steering wheel hard with the palm of his hand.

"God damn it," he said. Quickly he got the car parked at the curb, and went after Helen into the park. He had to trot to catch up to her.

When he caught her arm, she turned to face him. At least she was smiling.

"Well, Professor Shaw, I believe you're stalking me! But why would you chase after a crazy person, on such a nice December day?"

"I don't think you're crazy," Simon said. "And please call me Simon. When you say 'Professor Shaw,' I think of my father."

"Okay," she said, "if you call me Helen."

"I'm concerned about you."

"Let me guess. You got rid of me as fast as you could, and now you feel guilty."

"Yeah, I guess so. And, well . . ."

"What?"

"You don't look well."

"I should never go out without my lipstick," she said, laughing. "But I'm okay, honest. Heading home tomorrow." She looked better when she laughed, but Simon was still worried. He felt some responsibility for her state of mind.

"What are you going to do?"

"About Annie? Don't have a clue. Other than that, spend Christmas with my parents, go back to work, try to figure out what to do about Henry."

"Henry?"

"My poor boyfriend. Little does he know. I expect I have to tell him about Annie before I accept the ring, if I accept the ring. But look, you go on, do whatever you were planning to do today, I'll finish my walk, and I hereby absolve you from any responsibility for me, okay?"

"Fine," Simon said.

He walked back to his car, but he didn't stop thinking about Helen. He looked back at her. At first, he didn't see her. Then he noticed her red sweater. She was prone on the ground.

He didn't remember running to her. He just remembered getting there, dropping to her side, and feeling for a pulse. She had one, thank goodness. He reached into his jacket pocket. Damn it! His cell phone was in his car. How long would it take to get help? He'd have to run back to his car to call 911.

A jogger dropped on his knees next to them.

"I'm a doctor," he said. He took Helen's pulse, listened to her heart with an ear pressed to her chest, and pried open one eyelid.

"I think she's just fainted," he said. "What's her name?"

"Helen," Simon said.

"Helen," the doctor shouted into her ear. "Helen, wake up!"

Helen stirred.

"Help me lean her over and put her head down," the doctor said.

Helen regained consciousness quickly. She rubbed her face with her hands.

"What happened?" she asked.

"You fainted," Simon said.

"I'm a doctor," the jogger said. "Could you be pregnant?"

"Absolutely not, no way," Helen said.
"Do you have diabetes, heart disease?"
"No."
"Did you have breakfast this morning?"
"Afraid not. I've had a bit of a shock, too."
"Aha," the jogger said, handing her his water bottle. "That's it, then. Drink some of this. I haven't touched it yet."
Helen sipped a little water. She looked much better. The pace of Simon's own heart slowed with relief.
"Get a bite to eat, and rest for the afternoon. If you still don't feel well, go to the emergency room." The doctor resumed his run, waving at them as he jogged over the nearest hill.
"What shock?" Simon asked.
"You see that house?" she said, pointing to a large nineteenth-century brick house, beautifully restored, that stood just inside the park. "I've seen that house before many times. And I've never been here in my life. This life, that is. This house is in the compound where Annie lived." She looked around. "Where are the rest of the buildings?"
"That's the only one left. It's the Brevard House. The last remaining structure of the old Raleigh Christian Orphanage," Simon

said. “I think it was a boys’ dormitory.” As he said it, he knew he hadn’t finished with Helen Williams, or with Annie Evans.

4

> The body of Benjamin Franklin, printer (like the cover of an old book, its contents torn out and stripped of its lettering and gilding) lies here, food for worms, but the world shall not be lost, it will appear once more in a new and more elegant edition . . . revised and corrected by the author.
>
> — BENJAMIN FRANKLIN

"An orphanage," Helen said. "Not a boarding school, an orphanage."

Simon remembered the rough sketch she'd given him yesterday. He'd driven around with it in his jacket pocket all morning, trying to recall why he was familiar with its horseshoe-shaped configuration of buildings. He produced the map and pointed out the boundaries of the Orphanage to Helen.

"When you gave this sketch to me, it was oriented so that the open part of the campus faced toward me, which one assumes is south. Actually, we should look at it this way, with the open part of the horseshoe to the east." He pointed out the landmarks he now recognized. "To the east of the campus is Glenwood Avenue, where the main entrance of the Orphanage used to be. To the west is St. Mary's Street, right over there, he said, pointing back toward the street where he'd left his car. "This park was part of its grounds. Back then the Orphanage was on the edge of the city of Raleigh. Streets and buildings bordered it to the south. The Orphanage property was sold years ago, and I remember reading about it in a feature article in the newspaper. There was an aerial photograph of the grounds illustrating the article, and that's why your drawing looked familiar to me."

"This is bad news," she said.

"Why?" he said. "I thought you wanted some explanation . . ."

"I've never heard of the Raleigh Christian Orphanage. I don't want evidence this was a real place. I want proof I'm an overimaginative neurotic so I can go home and live like a regular person."

Her hands holding the drawing trembled, and it seemed to Simon that she swayed slightly. He took her by the elbow.

"Come on," he said. "Let's get some food into you. There's got to be a reasonable explanation for this. We just have to find it, that's all."

"You're going to help me?"

"Yeah, I'm going to help you."

The diner across the street from North Carolina State University served breakfast twenty-four hours a day. At first, Helen just picked at her scrambled eggs, but then, as her color improved, she polished off her eggs and buttered grits and drained a large glass of orange juice. Simon pushed his half-finished waffles and bacon over to her and she cleaned that up, too. Simon liked a woman who would eat. Diets annoyed him, especially in public, where they kept happy diners from enjoying their meals.

Helen looked much better after breakfast. She sat up straight in her chair, pushed her hair behind her ears, and smiled to the waitress when she brought them more coffee. Simon silently admonished himself for noticing how pretty she was. The last thing he needed was to be attracted to her. He was new at this client thing, but he understood that he needed to keep the relationship professional.

"How many meals did you say you missed?" Simon said.

"I don't really remember. I've had so

much on my mind, I couldn't think about food."

"I'm sorry if I upset you yesterday," Simon said. "I'm usually not rude."

"It's okay. What could I expect? That you would rush over to my hotel room, elated because you'd discovered proof of reincarnation in just twenty-four hours? I was impressed you'd showed up in person, instead of blowing me off over the telephone."

"That was no excuse."

"Okay, I forgive you. Now explain."

"Explain what?"

"You said back there in the park that you were sure there was a reasonable explanation for all this. Let's have it. I've been waiting for it for years." She crossed her arms expectantly, teasing him.

"The most obvious reason you thought you'd seen that building before, is that you have seen it, and forgotten it. And somewhere, somehow, you learned about the Orphanage. I have a psychologist friend who calls it cryptoamnesia."

"Yeah, I know. I've read about it."

"Are you sure you've never been to Raleigh before? You must have. It's the state capital."

"I've been over my whole life with a fine-toothed comb. I've talked to my teachers, my childhood friends, my parents, at least my father, as recently as two weeks ago. I can't talk to my mother about this. She cries whenever I bring it up. She's afraid I'm mentally ill. Anyway, of course I've visited Raleigh. Once when I was six I came to the state fair. Then there was the mandatory sixth-grade field trip to the legislature and the state museums. For two summers, my family rented a cottage on Kerr Lake, and each time we came into Raleigh once, for dinner and a movie. The second summer we saw *E.T.* I pretended my baby doll, Mary Alice, was an alien for weeks afterward. That's the sum of my acquaintance with Raleigh."

"What about history projects, or history courses? Maybe you read something about the Orphanage. . . ."

"I hated history. Sorry," she said. "But I did. I thought it was so boring, not nearly as exciting as fiction. Besides, I went through all my history textbooks. And I've still got all my childhood story books — two bookcases full. I've checked them all. None of them feature an orphanage in Raleigh, or a woman who lived at the turn of the century, or anything similar. I was heavy into the Bobbsey Twins and horses at the age of eight."

"Was that how old you were when these memories surfaced?"

"My mother says I first mentioned them to her when I was eight, but I feel like I've always had them."

The waitress stopped at their table.

"Want me to take this for you, shug?" she asked, tapping at the bill still lying on the table near Simon's elbow. Simon saw the long line of customers waiting at the cash register, coveting their booth.

"We'd better go," he said. "My house is just around the corner. We can talk more there."

"Nice place," Helen said.

"Thanks," Simon said. He took her coat and hung it in the closet off the living room.

"Really nice," she said, taking in the Oriental rugs, leather sofa and chairs, china cabinet filled with gleaming silver and crystal, and the gilt-framed paintings hanging on Simon's walls. His living room and dining room formed an el and took up most of the space on the first floor of the house, a Craftsman-style bungalow. A door off the dining room led down a short hall to a tiny bathroom, galley kitchen, and screened porch off the back of the house.

"My boyfriend has an enormous entertainment center and one sofa in his living room, and a mattress on the floor of his bedroom. He lives out of boxes. It's not that he can't afford better, he just doesn't care."

"I was an only child, so I inherited all my parents' things after they died. What's the point of having it if I don't use it?"

Helen plinked a few keys on the baby grand piano in the corner of the living room.

"Do you play?" she asked.

"I've been working on *Für Elise* for ten years, if you call that playing," Simon said. "My mother played wonderfully, at least it seemed so to me."

Simon flicked on the gas fire while Helen settled into the leather sofa.

"Let me find my notebook," Simon said. He sifted through the folders and books in his briefcase, which leaned open against the coffee table, and pulled out a narrow reporter's notebook. He skimmed a few pages, then wrote a few more lines in it.

Helen felt inestimably comforted watching him. Her instincts told her that she'd finally found the one person who might be qualified, temperamentally and professionally, to help her. She prayed he wouldn't become frustrated and quit, like everyone else she'd entrusted her problem to.

"Okay," Simon said. "Let's review this. Stop me if I make any errors." He flipped the pages of his notebook while he talked.

"You've had memories of a past life almost as long as you can remember," Simon said. "Those pages of memories you gave me, is that all you remember?"

"Yes, the memories are just flashes. Not a complete life."

"Like a door that's ajar."

"Exactly. I just get a glimpse. That's part of what frustrates me. I don't understand what I do remember. And what I do remember scares me."

"You've consulted psychologists and such."

"Yes, and they've sent reports to Wade. He can tell you that I appear to be normal."

"I don't think Wade can share any of that with me," Simon said. "Patient confidentiality and all that."

"I'll sign a waiver."

"Okay. I'll talk to him later. So, you've thoroughly investigated your own past, and you can't find any trace of an influence, like a book or a movie, that might have planted these memories."

"No. Of course, maybe I missed something. I hope I missed something."

"And you've never spent any time in Raleigh, except for trip to the state fair, a school field trip, and a couple of summers at Kerr Lake."

"Exactly." Simon stared at the fire, tapping his pen on the notepad.

"Well," she said. "What now?"

"There are bound to be records of the Raleigh Christian Orphanage. It was a big institution, and it operated for seventy-five years. When the Orphanage shut down and the property was sold, all the money went to a sister organization, the Raleigh Christian Foundation. I expect they have the Orphanage archives."

"You haven't said what you really think," she said.

"About what?"

"About, well, you know. The chance that I might be . . ."

"Best to say it out loud. The reincarnation of a turn-of-the-century orphanage matron? It doesn't matter what I think. Research is about facts, not preconceptions, otherwise I'll just find the evidence that supports what I already believe."

Helen stood up to leave, so Simon got her coat and helped her into it.

"I'm going over to Wade's office to sign a waiver so the two of you can talk about me behind my back," she said.

"Okay," Simon said. "I'll call him in a little bit and see when we can get together." Simon picked his car keys off a table near the door.

"I want to walk," Helen said. "It's not far."

Simon stood on his front stoop and jangled his keys as he watched her walk away from him. After she went around the corner, he turned to go inside and noticed a binder protruding from his mailbox.

Marcus was nothing if not thorough. The summary of reincarnation research he'd promised Simon was comprehensive, compelling, and single-spaced. Simon skimmed it while standing on his porch, then went back inside. He sat down with a Coke to reread the text.

Marcus recapped what he had already told Simon — that no reputable scholarly authority believed that individuals who "remembered" past lives were anything but suggestible, disturbed people who manufactured memories from a jumble of sources and delivered them to gullible researchers or manipulative therapists. To reinforce his adamancy, he had added three pages of references and footnotes to support his conclusions. Simon read through them: They were unassailably authoritative, books and journal articles by prominent psychologists and researchers. Simon had to accept their conclusions. How could he do otherwise? Despite what he'd told Helen about staying objective, how could any reasonable person believe in reincarnation? He was certain that he'd not lived a previous life, and he'd never experienced anything that remotely suggested to him that those who died weren't gone for good. Maybe their souls existed somewhere else, he could admit to that possibility, but they weren't here.

Simon's phone rang. "Julia" flashed through his mind, but he dismissed it. He hadn't talked to her in weeks. He lifted the receiver.

"Hello," Julia said. Simon, surprised, didn't answer immediately.

"Are you there?" she asked.

"Sure," Simon said. "Yes. What's up?"

"I'm sorry to bother you with this," she said, "but I think I might have left my diamond earrings at your house. I've looked everywhere else for them, and the last time I remember wearing them was when I went to that faculty dinner at Kenan with you."

And came home with Simon and spent the night. And the next day, and the following night also. Simon remembered that weekend very well.

"I changed my clothes in your guest bedroom, and I may have put my earrings in that little box on the dresser to keep them safe."

"I'll look."

"You don't have to right this minute. Just when you get a chance."

"No, I'll look now. Hang on."

Sure enough, the solitaire studs twinkled in the light when he opened the lacquer box on the guest room dresser. He picked up his upstairs extension.

"They're here," Simon said.

"Thank God," Julia said. "My grandparents gave them to me when I got my law degree. I'd hate to lose them."

"Want me to bring them over?"

"No, no. I'll come by sometime and get them. I still have a key, if you're not home. And that'll give me a chance to return the key, too. I'll leave it in your mailbox."

"Good," Simon said. He couldn't think of anything else to say.

"Have a nice Christmas."

"I will. You, too."

Julia's phone call gave Simon a couple of things to ruminate upon. His single status, for one, and how he hated living alone. For another, his premonition that Julia was on the phone when it rang. Did that qualify as a psychic event? He supposed it did, along with turning on a radio and finding it playing the same song he'd been humming, or knowing what was in a birthday package before opening it, or who was at the door when someone knocked. These small telepathic events happened to everyone. He'd read an article about psychic events in *Scientific American*, and hadn't been surprised that the authors concluded that telepathy and precognition were verifiable phenomena, well documented in a number of scientific studies, although no one had any idea what mechanism powered them. Very little was known about the human brain, after all, and who knew what powers it had that hadn't been explained?

If he accepted these small psychic events as real phenomena, how did belief in reincarnation differ? Since reincarnation wasn't acceptable to the Western secular understanding of how the world worked, did that alone mean it wasn't true, or even that it shouldn't be considered?

A tiny prickle of unease settled between Simon's shoulder blades. As he read more of Marcus' notes, the prickle evolved into a full-fledged shiver of doubt.

"You might as well know this," Marcus

had penciled at the top of the next page. "There are thousands of cases of children remembering past lives that don't fall into any of the categories I previously described."

According to Marcus, Dr. Ian Stevenson, Director of Personality Studies at the University of Virginia, had devoted forty years to the scientific documentation of past-life memories (without hypnosis) of children from all over the world. He had over three thousand cases on file. Stevenson collected most of his data from children in countries where people believed in reincarnation, but had a substantial number of recollections from the West. In all his cases, the children's "past lives" were not remarkable in any way. Most remembered being fishermen, or housewives, or small merchants. The children, and their families, had nothing to gain from perpetrating a hoax. In fact, Stevenson found twenty-five cases in Burma where children claimed to remember past lives as Japanese soldiers. They exhibited characteristics such as food preferences and social attitudes common to the Japanese. To find out that their child was the reincarnation of an Imperial soldier was the last thing any Burmese family would want.

Stevenson had answers for any objection. Why doesn't everyone remember a past life? Because, Stevenson believes, we're not supposed to remember. The only individuals who return to the next incarnate's memory were those who died unexpectedly, leaving important unfinished business behind. Stevenson also proposed that a person's past life could explain phobias, addictions, talents, unusual aptitudes, untaught skills, and differences between twins. Even physical problems, such as illnesses, could leave their marks on subsequent incarnations. In one case, a young child interviewed by Stevenson insisted that a birthmark on his back was the scar left by the sword that ended his previous life. Simon couldn't suspend his disbelief enough not to laugh out loud at the birthmark story. How convenient, Simon thought, that belief in reincarnation solves so many problems in psychology, psychiatry, biology, and medicine. He glanced at the long, white scar on his forearm. He remembered burning himself while trying to iron a shirt, but, who knew? He had to chuckle.

The cases Stevenson studied were compelling, but Simon supposed that his mind was just too corrupted by a Western secular education to make the leap of faith required to believe in the reincarnation of souls. It was bogus, had to be. Human beings would go to almost any length to explain away mortality and envision an afterlife. Even Neanderthals sprinkled their dead with red ocher and flowers, and left stone tools in their graves for use in heaven.

December dusk had fallen. The living room was quite dark, except for the circle of light thrown by his reading lamp and the glow of the gas fire. A dark form leaped from behind the sofa and onto Simon's lap, startling him.

"I see now why black cats were burned at the stake during the Middle Ages. You shouldn't creep about so."

Simon's other two cats appeared at his feet. One rubbed his leg, and the other, who Simon swore was fathered by a Siamese, let out a high-pitched wail.

"Okay," Simon said. "I realize it's past your dinnertime. I was busy."

Each cat had her own bowl in the utility room. He dished up a little cat food, but mostly leftovers, for them. Scraps were good for cats, and dogs, too. He didn't care what veterinarians said. Who wanted to eat the same damn thing every day? Especially if it was "scientifically formulated." He'd grown up around dozens of animals —

dogs, cats, pigs, and cattle — and he never heard of any of them dying of scraps poisoning. Commercial pet food was invented after World War II by meat processors looking to make a profit off meat byproducts. Up until then, pets were doing just fine without it. The pet food industry was part of a worldwide conspiracy, Simon figured, just the first stage toward feeding human beings carefully designed formulas in cans. The food police's most recent move was the bold decree that hamburgers could not be served rare. Simon fought it at every opportunity.

He checked his refrigerator. Except for a six-pack of Coke and a few condiments, it was bare. One of his friends needed to have a party so he could stock up. It seemed he'd have to order a pizza, or go out and eat alone. Neither appealed to him.

He thought of Dr. Wade Ferrell. If he was still at his office, he might be up for eating out. Then Simon could pick his brain about Helen Williams.

"You caught me with my keys in my hand," Ferrell said. "I almost didn't answer the phone. I'll meet you at Players Retreat in ten minutes."

Simon got there first and settled down at a pine table in a corner. The PR hadn't changed much in years. Same Wolfpack-red sports decor, same food, same pool table, same bar, same mechanical games, new juke box playing the same oldies.

Dr. Wade Ferrell slipped onto the chair opposite Simon and picked up a grease-spattered menu.

"I'm not taking you away from your family?" Simon asked.

"Not at all. I'm enjoying the lull before the storm. My wife's at our beach house preparing for Christmas — we're having both kids, their spouses, and five grandkids this year."

"Sounds hectic, and wonderful."

"It's busy. Organization helps, and Susan is great at it. She has her lists and such. The shopping's been done for months. All I have to do is buy her a gift, pick up a tree at the farmers' market, and get down there. Tree selection and decoration is my responsibility."

Both men knew what they wanted without looking at the menu. The waitress, who was over sixty and had been waiting tables there since Wade was an undergraduate at N.C. State, swiftly wrote their order for two double chili cheeseburgers, fried onion rings, and draft beer.

The beer arrived instantly, and both men

quaffed down half a glass.

"Man, that's good," Ferrell said.

"Busy day?"

"Sort of. People's complaints change around the holidays. I call it 'the Christmas malaise' — part rhinovirus, part excitement, part depression. I recommend avoiding those stupid magazines and TV shows that tell you how to have the perfect Christmas. Most everybody lives to January."

Ferrell was his drug representatives' dream. Not for him the stoic, biofeedback, physical therapy, lose weight and eat right way to health. He liked medicine. "They're just chemicals, they can't hurt you," he once said to Simon, while dumping a handful of pill samples into his lap. "Try some of these, see if they help."

Ferrell was overweight, garrulous, and work-addicted. He had more fun being a doctor than Bill Gates had being rich. Tonight Wade's necktie sported a Santa's happy face, with a red light bulb in its nose that Simon was sure could be controlled from somewhere in Ferrell's pocket, to the delight of his youngest patients.

Their cheeseburgers and onion rings were deliciously greasy and satisfying.

"I take it," Ferrell said, wiping his mouth

with a napkin the size of a dish towel, "that you want to talk to me about Helen Williams."

"Yeah," Simon said. "She said she's had some psychologists' reports sent to you?"

"Right," Ferrell said. "All that's unusual psychologically about Helen are her past-life memories."

"All? Believing she's lived an earlier life is a little more than 'all.' "

"Is it? What's important is, can she live a normal life and still experience these memories? In psychiatric lingo, can she integrate them? Well, she can't. She's afraid to get married because of one specific memory, that of burying a baby. I could care a whit if what she remembers is 'true' or 'false'."

"But you're a scientist!"

"Just hold on, there. Medicine is not a science, it's an art."

"Sure, I forgot."

"Western science wears blinders when it comes to any sort of psychic puzzle. The mind is supposed to be one hundred percent the product of a physical brain. Okay, so how does the brain explain consciousness, love, whatever? Where is mental space? Is a living brain necessary to the existence of a mind?"

"Oh, come on!"

"The scientific establishment insists that people are just genes influenced by their environment. Nothing more. Do you believe that?"

"I don't know."

"At least you're honest. I'm a doctor, I have a patient whom I've known since she was a baby, I know she's not crazy, and she can't sleep at night. I want her to be able to sleep at night. That's all I'm interested in."

"Where do I come in?"

"You find out if Annie Evans ever lived. If she did, okay. If not, okay. I think Helen can deal with either. It's the uncertainty that she can't live with."

"But surely you don't believe in reincarnation, do you?"

"I've been practicing medicine for almost thirty years. Nothing surprises me anymore."

5

> Minds are not brains, but users of brains.
>
> — DR. IAN STEVENSON

Simon's house was dark, chilly, and unwelcoming. When he turned on his lights, the string of Christmas lights draped across his mantel instantly lit up, improving the atmosphere a bit. But the poinsettia the college had sent was already losing its lower branches, and one of the blue candles in his menorah had toppled over. Maybe he should have set up a Christmas tree after all, Simon thought. He was glad he was going to Marcus' home for Christmas dinner. He reminded himself that he had chosen to stay home for the holidays and avoid the cascade of emotion that he felt whenever he spent time with either side of his family. If he was lonely, it was his own damn fault. Remember this next year, he thought, and make a different choice.

Upstairs, Simon went into his study to pass the time until he could reasonably go to bed. He sat down at his desk and mashed the play button on his CD player, which contained a rock 'n' roll Christmas disk. Madonna singing "Santa, Baby" improved his mood.

For want of anything better to do, Simon typed "Raleigh Christian Orphanage" into an Internet search engine. Idly he waited for a selection of blue-lettered, obscure, probably useless references to appear on his screen. To his surprise, the first entry was anything but. It led him to the Raleigh Christian Orphanage Alumni Association home page. Over the years, hundreds of people must have graduated from the Orphanage's high school, but it hadn't occurred to him that they would stay in touch with each other. But of course they would. These people had shared their childhoods and adolescence.

The one-page Web site displayed the name, address, and phone number of the alumni association president. Frank Webb lived in University Park, down Hillsborough Street a few blocks and across the street from State, not far from Simon's own neighborhood. Simon called the man immediately.

Webb was eager to talk with Simon, who concocted a feasible story about researching the orphanage movement in the early part of the twentieth century without mentioning Helen Williams. Webb accepted his fib without question, which made Simon feel a bit ashamed. Detecting, he'd learned, sometimes required duplicity.

"I've got lots of material," Webb said. "Photos, letters, and I wrote a book on the history of the Orphanage. It's not a real book, not published, I mean. I typed it up myself. I've got a copy I can lend you."

Webb, who told Simon that he was a retired engineer, invited Simon to come by his house after lunch the next day.

Simon hung up, elated, then resisted the impulse to call Helen. He wanted to investigate her problem alone, at least at this juncture, to keep her from distracting him. He liked Helen more and more, but she was planning to marry someone else, and he wanted to avoid romantic disappointments. Best that he treat her case as just another academic puzzle.

Simon was relieved the next morning when he approached his office, with a cold Coke and a doughnut in one hand and his briefcase in another, and didn't see any students waiting outside. Students who came to office hours just a few days before the exams were of two desperate varieties. The first were flunking. The second were overachievers who were worried they weren't going to get an A. He spent most of these sessions reassuring both species that the sky wasn't falling.

Simon unlocked the door to his office and dumped his briefcase on his desk. Then he saw the folded paper lying on the floor in front of the door. He opened it with a heavy heart. It was written in tiny, cramped, almost illegible script on a page torn crookedly from a yellow legal pad.

"Dear Professor Simon," it read, *"I see that you are teaching a course on writing history. You've got to let me take it. I'm making lousy grades on all my papers. It's stupid that an accounting major has to take any liberal arts courses anyway. I'm sure your class is already full of suck-ups, but my father donated ten thousand dollars to the capital campaign, so I think I deserve some extra consideration. — Andy Haight"*

Simon stuck Haight's note in the file with the rest of his fellow petitioners. Then he unfolded two envelopes of Goody's Powders and dumped them into his Coke can, stirring the mixture with a pen. He drank it while checking his e-mail, which, mercifully, contained only spam.

Sophie Berelman rapped at Simon's open door before waddling into his office. She lowered herself slowly into the chair in front of Simon's desk. Her long, frizzy dark hair was pulled back into a ponytail. She shoved her cat's-eye-shaped glasses up the bridge of her nose with an index finger.

"I'm hiding from Vera," Sophie said. "She's in the faculty lounge. She gives me such disapproving looks. I guess I'm supposed to be at home, knitting tiny garments, embracing my confinement. In her day, women waited discreetly at home until their babies were born."

"How much longer do you have?" Simon asked.

"A couple of weeks," she said. "But I've got exam week covered, just in case. I feel like a stuffed sausage."

"I think you look great," Simon said, with the male animal's sense of pride in the consequences of sex.

"I understand," Sophie said, "that you're investigating a past-life story."

"What a disreputable notion," Simon said. "Where did you hear that?"

"Marcus. But don't worry, I won't tell anyone else."

"I'm just trying to help a friend of a

friend," Simon said "Naturally, it's a ridiculous idea."

Sophie shifted her weight, resting her hands on her stomach and crossing her legs at the ankles.

"Oh, I don't know," she said. "Hasidic Jews believe in reincarnation. It's called *gilgul ha-neshamot* in Hebrew."

"I thought Judaism didn't have an afterlife dogma."

"You know this from your extensive study of the subject?" she said. Once Sophie had learned that Simon's mother was Jewish, she'd campaigned relentlessly for him to learn something about his heritage. "It's not going to go away," she'd say. "Why don't you find out what you're missing?"

"Different branches of Judaism have different notions about the afterlife," she went on. "The disciple of Jewish reincarnation theology is Rabbi Gershom. He's documented hundreds of cases of past-life memories of the Holocaust. And others have documented hundreds more."

"You can't believe in it," Simon said.

Sophie shrugged. "I don't know what I believe," she said. "I suppose I should think it's a kind of hysteria, a psychological remnant of the Jewish experience during the Holocaust. Except that some of the folks who remember traveling on trains to Auschwitz are gentiles who live in places like Nebraska. They have no connection to Eastern Europe or the Jewish experience."

She shifted her weight again.

"Do you want some references?" she asked. "I've got a file someplace."

"No thanks," Simon said. "I have enough questions to answer as it is."

Sophie levered herself out of the chair.

"If you change your mind, you know where to find me," she said.

Simon's office hours crawled by. No traumatized students dropped in, and he had nothing pressing to do. He filed. He tidied. He wrote some end-of-the-year checks to his favorite charities. He called the synagogue to find out what day of Hanukkah it was, only to learn it didn't even start for another week. He didn't care. He'd light all the candles again tonight anyway.

"You know," the rabbi had said to Simon before he rang off, "we have a Jewish religion and life class starting after the first of the year. You should come. It might interest you."

"Thanks," Simon said, "but I'm comfortable being confused."

"Are you sure?"

Simon didn't answer, but thanked the rabbi for his interest. He wasn't comfortable, but he lacked the resolution to do anything about it.

At last, noon came and he could leave his office and wander down to the faculty lounge. Marcus and Jack were already there, eating little hot dogs simmered in barbecue sauce, ham biscuits, scoops of chicken and rice casserole, chips and dip, and brownies.

"Judy brought this in," Jack said. "The firemen down at the Oberlin Road station had their Christmas party last night."

Simon helped himself.

"By the way," Simon said to Marcus, between bites, "thanks for breaking my confidence and telling Sophie about my project."

"He told me, too," Jack said. "Very interesting."

"I felt you needed all the assistance you could get," Marcus said. "How were the notes I left you?"

"Excellent," Simon said. "What do you make of those cases of children's past-life memories?"

"Don't know," Marcus said.

"You must have an opinion," Simon said.

Marcus shrugged. "I don't think those kids have been reincarnated, if that's what you want to know. Can I explain their memories? No, I can't."

"You know," Jack said. "There was, and still is, widespread belief in reincarnation among Native Americans."

"I don't want to hear about it," Simon said.

Jack ignored him. "The Dakota teach that man is reincarnated, and that between lives, he lives with the Gods and gets instruction in magic and healing."

"The mythology hasn't been corrupted? How early has it been documented?" Marcus asked.

"Strachey reported it amongst the Powhatan in Virginia in 1612, and the Jesuit record of Huron soul and rebirth concepts dates from 1632. I can get you some references, if you like," Jack said to Simon.

"Please, no," Simon said. "Not that. Not references."

Frank Webb opened his door as Simon was walking up the front path to his house. Webb was a neatly dressed man in his late seventies. He wore a blue-and-white-striped polo shirt, polyester self-belted slacks, and white athletic shoes. The path of a comb through hair cream made neat rows in his thinning hair.

"Welcome," Webb said. "We've just finished lunch. Can I get you anything?"

"I've eaten, thanks," Simon said.

"How about coffee and a slice of fruitcake?" His wife asked. The Webbs were a matched set. She wore a blue wool skirt to mid-calf, sensible canvas shoes, and a white-and-blue-striped blouse with a gold initial pin at the throat. Her graying dark hair was pulled back from her forehead with a blue velvet headband.

"You have to try Nancy's cake," Webb said. "It's not like those bricks that pass for fruitcake that you buy in the grocery store."

Simon didn't have a choice. Nancy had already vanished through a swinging door into the kitchen, where he heard dishes clattering.

Webb ushered Simon into a tiny room lined with mismatched bookcases. Photographs, books, scrapbooks, and boxes filled the shelves. A desk, chair, and small sofa crowded the center of the room.

"Since I've retired, I've taken over the den as my office. Nancy said I might as well, saves my stuff from being scattered all over the house."

Simon took a seat on the sofa, while Webb swiveled his desk chair around to face him.

"I've been the president of the Orphanage's alumni association for thirty years," Webb said. "And I'm writing the history of my army regiment in Italy during World War II. Here's my book about the Orphanage," Webb said. With obvious pride, he handed Simon a thick typescript in a three-inch binder. "It's all in there," he said. "Took me two years to write this. If you're interested in the Orphanage, you won't need to go to the library. I've already done all the research. Are you looking for any particular information?"

"I have a friend," Simon said. "She's come across a reference to a person in some family papers. Has some reason to believe that this person may have worked at the Orphanage at the turn of the century."

"What was her name?"

"Annie Evans."

"Certainly. Miss Annie. She was the matron of the Baby Cottage from, let's see, 1909 or so until she left in 1930."

"Really?" Simon said. He was so taken aback he couldn't think of anything else to say.

"Want to see her picture?"

"Yes, please," Simon said. Webb took the binder from Simon's lap and leafed through it. "Here," he said, turning it to face Simon.

"Here's her picture. I photocopied it from the *Raleigh Christian Messenger*, the little magazine published by the group that sponsored the Orphanage. It was taken right after she was hired."

Annie looked steadily and calmly at the camera. She was a stocky woman, with dirty blond hair pulled sharply back, dressed in dark Victorian widow's weeds. Her hands were crossed in her lap, and she wore no jewelry except a wedding ring. She sat in a straight-back chair. Light from a window outside the frame fell on one side of her face. Simon could imagine that the picture was taken in her new employer's office, and that she'd never had a photograph taken before.

"Well," Simon said, still at a loss for words.

Nancy rescued him when she came in with a tray loaded with coffee and cake. Frank was right. The fruitcake was delicious — moist, dense, replete with fruits and nuts, and soaked with bourbon.

"This is wonderful," Simon said.

"There's a secret ingredient," Nancy said. "I don't give the recipe out to anybody."

Simon spent the next few minutes eating and sipping coffee, recovering his composure, while the Webbs talked about themselves.

"We met and fell in love at the Orphanage," Webb said. "You know, people think of bad things when they think of orphanages, but this one was a godsend for us both. My father died of pneumonia in 1934, and my mother couldn't take care of us. My brother and me were safe and secure at the Orphanage. We both graduated from high school, went into the service, and got good jobs when we got out."

"My father was a sharecropper," Nancy said. "He and my mother had seven children. We lived in a two-room house infested with red bugs. I've got an old picture of my sisters and me wearing flour-sack dresses. After my parents died of tuberculosis, my sisters and I were separated between two orphanages, here and the one at Oxford. My brothers took jobs. If I'd been raised at home, I sure wouldn't have finished high school. At the Orphanage, I took piano lessons and learned etiquette, then after I graduated I went to secretarial school."

"My mother tried to take me and my brother out of the place after she remarried," Webb said. "But we wouldn't leave. Her new husband wanted us to work in his sawmill. I wasn't about to quit high school, eat corn mush, and use an outhouse ever again if I didn't have to."

"You never knew Annie?" Simon asked.

"I arrived at the Orphanage after she'd left," Webb said.

"Can you think of anyone who might be alive who would remember her when she worked there?" Simon asked.

"Lorena Henly might. She's the oldest alumni — she graduated in 1921. She hasn't come to the last few reunions, but she's still living, last I heard."

"Who was the girl Miss Annie went to work for? Isn't her brother still alive?" Nancy asked.

"Stella Grimes," Webb said. "I forget her married name. She's been dead for years. But her brother is still going strong, in his nineties. He wasn't ever at the Orphanage, but he likes to keep in touch with the alumni."

"I expect Professor Shaw must be very confused," Nancy said.

"You see," Webb said, "Stella's mother left her at the Orphanage when her husband died. Like so many widows, she couldn't support a child. She went to Virginia, remarried, and came back to get Stella. She and her new husband had a son, Stella's half-brother, Fred. Her new husband was wealthy; I forget how he made his money. Anyway, they settled in Raleigh. Fred can tell you all about it."

"The story was," Nancy said, "that Miss Annie saved Stella's life. Stella took ill just a few days after arriving at the Baby Cottage and Miss Annie nursed her for weeks."

Frank leafed through the alumni directory.

"Here," he said, "Fred Grimes. He's over ninety. Now he lives in Florida during the winter. There's his phone number. You can have this copy of the alumni directory, too; call anyone you like. No one will mind."

Simon was reluctant to ask Webb his next question, but he knew he had to.

"Tell me," Simon said. "Has anyone else contacted you about Annie Evans recently?"

"No. Not many are interested in the Orphanage but us orphans, you might say."

"A young woman, attractive, with dark hair, hasn't come to see you about her? No one's written or called?"

"No," Frank said. "Why?"

"Just wondering."

"Of course, two copies of my book are deposited at the local history library," Webb said. "Anyone can read it there."

"Did you send copies to any other libraries?" Simon asked.

Webb shook his head. "Too expensive to photocopy," he said.

Simon dropped the Orphanage's alumni directory and Webb's book on his coffee table. He didn't even take off his coat before he had his telephone and the phone book in his hands, looking up the phone number of the Olivia Raney Local History Library.

The librarian who answered the phone recognized his name and eagerly answered Simon's questions.

"We're very careful about our manuscript collections here, Professor Shaw," she said. "Some of our materials are irreplaceable. Our copies of Mr. Webb's work can't be checked out. Anyone who wants to read it here and take notes can, but they've got to sign for it, and we keep their driver's license at the desk until the document is returned. All materials are accounted for before we close, every day."

"Can you tell me if a woman named Helen Williams has checked out Webb's book, say, in the last year?"

Simon heard the clacking of computer keys. "No one by that name has ever requested any materials in this library," she said. "And Mr. Webb's book has only been used twice in the last year, both times by graduate students, one from State and one from Duke."

"It's never been borrowed by another library?" Simon asked.

"Not since it was deposited here, six years ago," she said.

"Thanks very much," Simon said.

"Is this a new case of yours?" she asked. "I'd be so pleased to help you with anything you need."

Simon hastened to assure her otherwise. The last thing he needed was a leak.

Simon hung up the phone, still processing what he had learned. Annie Evans was a real person, and it seemed that Helen couldn't have found out about her from either Frank Webb or his book.

Webb's typescript contained little information about the early years of the Orphanage. It was more of a yearbook of the fifties and sixties, crammed with photos and reminiscences of proms, football games, first jobs, and alumni reunions.

Webb had gathered a few documents that did describe life in the Orphanage during its early years. In one letter to the *Raleigh Christian Messenger* dated in October 1905, the superintendent described the orphan's typical day to the readers of the little magazine, who, Simon assumed, contributed funds to the Orphanage through their churches.

The Orphanage bell rang at five thirty in the morning when the children began their day by building fires, getting water from the well, and fixing breakfast. The "cow boys" fed and milked the cows, the "big girls" cleaned and dusted the dormitories, other boys filled tubs of water for the washerwomen. At seven fifteen, the children ate breakfast, which was served by four of the bigger girls. The superintendent read the morning Bible lesson and led prayers before anyone could start eating. At eight fifteen the school-age children walked a mile and a quarter to school. At two thirty, they returned for dinner, then did their afternoon chores — cutting firewood, ironing and sewing, scrubbing floors, darning, plowing, peeling vegetables, putting up preserves. Playtime was from five to six o'clock, followed by another religious service, supper, and bedtime at 8 o'clock. Several nights a week, the children ate peanut butter and molasses sandwiches for supper.

Simon learned from the documents that there were no children under the age of five at the Orphanage until 1907, when Miss

Annie Evans was hired to be the matron at the Baby Cottage.

Simon paged through the alumni directory. Lorena Henly, the oldest living alumni of the orphanage, lived in Glenwood Towers, an apartment building for the elderly on Glenwood Avenue. But he decided to call Fred Grimes, Stella's brother, first.

Frank Webb had called Grimes already, so he was expecting to hear from Simon.

"It's the emphysema," Grimes said, his voice raspy but steady over the telephone from Florida. "All those years smoking cigarettes. Last two winters in Raleigh, I almost died. Now I live here from October to April. The rest of the year, I live with my daughter, Phoebe."

Simon started to speak, but Fred interrupted him.

"I know," Fred said. "You want to know about Annie Evans. She was my sister's housekeeper. Miss Evans was the matron of the Baby Cottage when my mother was forced to leave Stella at the Orphanage. Right after she left, Stella got measles. In those days, measles was a killer."

Simon grabbed his notebook to take notes.

"Miss Annie had already had the measles,

so she quarantined herself and Stella in the infirmary for two weeks, and Stella pulled through."

"Anyway, I will never forget the day my parents and I went back to the Orphanage to get Stella. I was six and Stella was eleven. She was the prettiest girl, with long curly blond hair and bright blue eyes, sweet as cherry pie. Anyway, Stella was real attached to everyone at the Orphanage, especially Miss Annie, so my parents decided to live in Raleigh to make the transition easier for her. My father made his money manufacturing windshield wipers for trolley cars up in Virginia. Here, he opened an auto parts business. We owned fifteen stores all over North and South Carolina by the time I sold the business. Anyway, after Stella got married, she asked Miss Annie to come be her housekeeper. That was, oh, 1930, the same year Stella had her son Joe. Are you following this?"

"Yeah, keep going," Simon said, scribbling quickly.

"Anyway, Stella died in 1980, and Joe and his wife a few years later in a car accident. A grandson, Jesse, is her only grandchild."

"Who?"

"Jesse. Jesse Lay. Joe's son. Jesse's a mess.

He's a womanizer and a playboy. My two children turned out better. My son's a stockbroker. He and his family live in New York City. You've heard of my daughter, Phoebe Hays, I suppose? You can hardly help it, if you live in Raleigh."

Simon had heard of her. Phoebe was politically connected. A former ambassador to the Dominican Republic, she and her husband entertained lavishly at their magnificent home in Hayes Barton.

"Jesse and Phoebe's son Lucius control the family business now. Keeping an eye on investments, if you call that work. Mostly Lucius runs for the Senate, and Jesse chases women."

Simon remembered Lucius Hays' last bid for the Republican nomination. He'd almost gotten it, and rumor was he would next time around.

"Can you think of anyone else who might have known Miss Annie? Someone I could talk to here in town? I already have Lorena Henly's name."

"Not from way back then. Later, yes. In fact, my family hired some kids from the Orphanage over the years. Oh, hell, I can't remember any names." The old man hemmed and hawed for a minute. "Let me have your e-mail address," Grimes said, "and if a name comes to me, I'll let you know. This is what I hate about being old. I remember too much about some things, and not enough about others. I carry around a little notepad so when I do think of something, I write it down right away. You call Phoebe, though, if you want to, tell her I said she was to talk to you if she gives you the brush-off."

The two men exchanged e-mail addresses and Simon rang off.

He debated trying to see Lorena Henly, but the woman was elderly and it was getting late in the day. He had to get to his eight o'clock date with the Bloomin' Book Club, which his neighbor, Greer Lysacht, had drafted him to attend. Simon didn't believe for one minute that the club members wanted to read *The South Between the World Wars*. He suspected they were mostly interested in his detecting.

Simon allowed his mind to drift to Helen. He couldn't make up his mind about her. She gave him the impression that she was intelligent, determined, vulnerable, and completely truthful. If she made up her story, how could she have found out about Annie Evans? What was her motive? If she wanted to concoct a past life, why not choose someone famous and important? If she was mentally ill, what would happen once she knew Evans was a real person? He tried to put her out of his mind when his doorbell rang.

Helen stood on his front porch.

"I was walking over to Cameron Village for dinner, and I thought I'd check to see if you were home. I owe you a meal, I believe."

Her gaze drifted past Simon and into his living room, where the telephone sat on top of the pile of documents he'd collected while talking to Grimes.

"You've found something," she said.

Simon's hesitation told her he had.

"What is it?" she said. "You've got to tell me."

Simon closed the door behind her, and gestured her to a seat on the sofa.

"I've found Annie Evans," he said.

"That's not funny," she said.

"I'm not joking. Here she is."

Simon showed her Annie's photo, and explained what information about her he had gathered. During the whole conversation, Helen sat straight up on the edge of the sofa, as if a broom handle were tied to her spine, with her right hand spread across her chest just below her throat. After he'd finished, she held Webb's book on her lap, open to Annie's picture.

"She doesn't look like me. It's silly, but I always thought she'd look like me." She began to laugh nervously, but then collected herself.

She looked at Simon. "I don't understand," she said. "I don't know what's happening. What does this mean?"

Simon sat down next to her.

"There must be a reasonable explanation," he said.

"You keep saying that."

They ordered Chinese takeout and went over all the material that Simon had collected that day. He watched her as carefully as he could without being too obvious. Not even by a flicker of an eyelash did she indicate that she knew the Webbs, had ever heard of Stella Grimes and her family, or had ever been near the local history library. Simon found it impossible to believe that she was consciously acting. If she was, she was a better actress than Bette Davis in *Dark Victory*.

"What do we do next?" she asked.

Simon outlined his plan to her. Tomorrow he'd interview Lorena Henly and Phoebe Hays, and hope that Fred Grimes remembered someone else he might talk to. Then he intended to locate the archives of the Orphanage and get permission from the foundation to go through them.

"There has to be a connection between you and this woman that you don't remember," Simon said. "Nothing else makes sense."

"I want to come with you," Helen said. "Especially to see Mrs. Henly. I mean, I could recognize her!"

Simon didn't think Helen was intentionally deceiving him, so there was no reason to keep her isolated from his work anymore. Perhaps something would jog a hidden memory, who knew?

"Of course," he said. "Give me a couple of hours in the morning to get in touch with people. I'll pick you up about ten."

Simon dropped Helen at her hotel before going to the Bloomin' Book Club, where he spent a delightful evening drinking wine with a room full of intelligent, attractive women, not one of whom was single. Some of them had even read his book.

6

> Now it happened that as Jesus was praying alone, the disciples were with him, and he asked them, "Who do the people say that I am?"
> And they answered, "John the Baptist, but others say Elijah; and others, that one of the old prophets has risen."
>
> — LUKE 9:18–19

"I never married," Lorena Henly said, "and I've never been sorry. Oh, I had lots of offers, but I saw what a married woman's life was like, and I wanted no part of it. My mother and my aunt both died in childbirth. That's how I ended up at the Orphanage. I was better off there, too."

Miss Henly was nearly blind and bent over from osteoporosis, but she moved around her tiny kitchen confidently, placing a plate of muffins, cups, sugar, cream, and a pot of tea on a tray. Only when she went to lift it did she hesitate.

"Please let me," Simon said, picking up the tray and carrying it to the table in the sitting area of Miss Henly's studio apartment.

She moved carefully across the room and sat in a rocker, first touching it briefly to make sure it was placed where she thought it was. She pulled a lilac and pink knitted afghan over her legs. "Just a teaspoon of sugar for me, dear," she said, sensing that it was Helen who leaned forward to pour. "I hope you like Earl Grey," she said, blowing on her tea to cool it. "It's my favorite. The muffins are store-bought, I'm sorry to say. I worked my whole life as a baker, but now it's not safe for me to use the stove."

She set her cup down on the table next to her rocker, feeling for a clear spot among the knickknacks that crowded it.

"Now, Professor Shaw, what can I do for you, and for you, Miss Williams? You said on the telephone that you were interested in the early history of the orphanage I grew up in?"

"We want to find out whatever we can about a woman who was the matron of the Baby Cottage, Miss Annie Evans. I'm working on a family history, and her name came up in a document I found. I want to know if she's a relative of mine," Helen said, easily spinning the white lie she and Simon had concocted.

"I remember Miss Annie," Miss Henly

said. "Though I never lived at the Baby Cottage. I was eight when I was sent to live at the Orphanage."

"What was she like?" Helen asked. "Do you know anything about her people?"

"She was kind, but not warm, if you take my meaning. You could say that she held back just a little, enough to keep part of herself private. I do know she went to work at the Orphanage after her husband died in a fire. I never heard that she had any other relatives."

Helen started. "A fire?" she said. "Are you sure?"

"Yes, of course. Everyone knew about it."

"Do you know where she came from?" Simon asked. "Was it near Raleigh?"

"It was so long ago," Miss Henly said, turning her face toward his voice. "If I ever knew, I don't remember anymore."

"What was it like growing up there?" Helen asked.

"I loved it," Miss Henly said. "The matrons were kind, there was plenty to eat, I had dozens of 'brothers and sisters' to play with. I got a brand-new pair of shoes the first winter, and a new pair every winter after that. Oh, we worked hard, but who didn't in those days?

"Baking bread was my chore. I was so

little when I first learned, I stood on a box at a long wooden table in the kitchen, up to my elbows in flour. We baked the bread in cast-iron, wood-burning ovens. The big boys chopped wood every afternoon, and the little ones would tote it inside and load the wood box every morning. That's one reason I liked baking — it was so warm in the kitchen. We made a double batch of bread on Saturday, because Sunday was a day of rest."

"Do you remember an orphan named Stella Grimes?" Simon asked.

"Yes, but I didn't know her well. I was several years older. She was pretty — I was jealous of her long curly blond hair. Her aptitude was for needlework, I believe, so she spent her chore time sewing and mending. She and Miss Annie were close. Miss Annie saved her life when she was a baby."

"We've heard that story," Simon said. "Later Annie went to work for Stella."

"I never saw Stella again after I graduated," Miss Henly said. "Her family turned out to be rich, you know. What was her husband's name?"

"Lay," Simon said.

"I got a job baking in the kitchen of the Sir Walter Hotel, so our paths didn't cross. Later, I went to work at the Holsum Bread

Bakery. There was a young man at the hotel who was too persistent in his attentions to me, if you get my meaning."

"If you do remember any more details about Annie, like her maiden name, or anything at all, would you call me?" Simon asked.

"Certainly," Miss Henly said. "Leave your phone number on that notepad on the kitchen counter. I can get Gloria next door to read it to me if I need to. But don't expect to hear from me. My memory's good for a person my age, but I never knew that much about Miss Annie. She kept to herself, like I said."

Before they left, Miss Henly asked Simon to push her rocker into the full sunlight that poured from a picture window into the apartment.

"I like to feel the heat on my face," Miss Henly said. "On a sunny day, it's like standing in front of a warm oven."

Phoebe and William Hays lived in a vast stone mansion set in the midst of an acre lot in a wealthy residential community in old Raleigh. Simon drove through landscaped grounds, up the long, brick-paved driveway, and parked in the parking court in front of the house. It looked like a Christmas feature for *Southern Living* magazine. An evergreen wreath tied with an elaborate red velvet bow hung in each window. A matching wreath hid half the front door. Gold lights hung like icicles from the roof. A lawn jockey, his African-American face and hands repainted white for political correctness, wore a gold bell around his neck. His welcoming lantern, held out at the entrance to the front walk, was draped with holly.

"Wow," Helen said, craning her neck upward, "this place looks like a castle."

Simon wouldn't have been surprised if a butler in formal attire had answered the door, bearing a silver salver to receive Simon's visiting card. Instead, a small Hispanic woman in street clothes, wiping her hands on a spotless white apron, beckoned them to come inside.

"Wait," she said in broken English, pointing toward a room to the left of the wide-paneled foyer. "I'll get Mrs. Hays."

They waited for some time, seated uncomfortably on a gilt settee upholstered in pink silk. A twelve-foot Christmas tree filled a corner of the formal parlor. Carefully hung with pink and green plaid bows, pink and green glass balls, and tiny white fairy lights, the tree coordinated with the room's decor. It was a decorator's creation, not a family effort.

"Mrs. Hays must be busy arranging flowers or playing bridge or something," Helen said.

"You don't give her enough credit," Simon said. "She's as politically ambitious as her son. I'll bet she's working the phones in an office somewhere."

Soon, Phoebe Hays entered and stretched out a hand to each of them in turn. She was fashionably thin, dressed in tailored trousers and a silk shirt. Her arms and neck dripped with gold jewelry. Rhinestone-encrusted reading glasses hung from a gold chain around her neck. Her hair was bright white and expertly cut, short and stacked.

"I'm so sorry," she said, sitting down on a gilt chair that matched the settee, "I was on the phone to Republican National Headquarters. My husband is on the Executive Committee. My son Lucius is running for the Senate next year, you know."

"So I hear," Simon said.

"And you," she said, "are Professor Simon Shaw. I've read about your exploits. My father called this morning and told me you might drop by."

Simon introduced Helen.

"Daddy tells me that you're researching a family history, Miss Williams, but I don't know how I can help you."

"Mr. Grimes couldn't remember the names of his sister's employees," Simon said. "He told me that your family often hired graduates of the Orphanage. We're trying to locate anyone who might remember Stella's housekeeper, Annie Evans."

"I think Miss Evans, who was a matron at the Raleigh Christian Orphanage when your aunt was living there, may have been a relative of mine," Helen said.

"My dear," Mrs. Hays said, "that was ages ago. I couldn't possibly remember everyone who worked for Aunt Stella. Why would I?"

"Does your family still possess any documents from that time?" Simon asked. "We need firm facts and dates, so we can locate records. Knowing her birthday, where she came from, what church she attended, or even her maiden name, could help us find out more about her."

"Possibly," Mrs. Hays said. "My father saves everything, I mean everything. When he closed down his weekend cottage twenty years ago after Aunt Stella died, he brought truckloads of stuff over here. Our attic is full of his furniture, books, and papers. He lives here, you know. He has a suite on the second floor. My son Lucius and his family live in the east wing, so you see, the house is beyond full."

"Could we go through the attic?" Helen asked. "We'd be very respectful of Mr. Grimes' things."

"I wish I could say yes," she said.

Then say it, Simon thought.

"But no, I can't allow it."

"It's terribly important to me, finding out about this woman, you can't imagine . . . ," Helen said.

"That attic is a disaster waiting to happen. It's so stuffed with piles upon piles of boxes, you can hardly walk around in it. I go up there twice a year to scatter mothballs and mouse poison. My father didn't give you permission to go through his things, did he?"

"No, Ma'am," Simon said. "He didn't mention it, but . . ."

"Oh," Mrs. Hays interrupted, ". . . here's my son, Lucius."

Lucius Hays entered the room as if he were playing to a bank of television cameras. The words "strode vigorously" came to Simon's mind. Tall and well dressed, with a hundred-dollar haircut, iron gray hair, and a dark blue suit, he certainly looked the part of a United States' senator.

"Excuse me," Hays said to his mother, "I didn't realize you still had company." He looked at Simon and Helen pointedly, as if to remind them that their time was up.

"This is Professor Simon Shaw and his friend Helen Williams," Mrs. Hays said. "They want to go through our attic looking for documents."

Hays was instantly on guard. "What documents?"

"It's a genealogy thing," his mother said.

"I think that a relative of mine worked at the Raleigh Christian Orphanage at the same time that Stella Grimes lived there," Helen said.

"Good heavens," Hays said, "that was a hundred years ago. I don't understand this genealogy craze myself, I mean, once people have been dead for years, why bother?"

"I'm reluctant to allow it," Mrs. Hays said.

"I agree," Hays said. "For a stranger, even a distinguished one such as Professor Shaw, to look through our personal history, well, I'm running for the Senate. What if one of our relatives turned out to be," he laughed, "say, a Yankee spy? You understand, I'm sure." He clapped Simon on the back.

Mrs. Hays looked at her watch without any attempt to conceal it, got to her feet, and shook both their hands, quickly.

"It was good of you to come by," Mrs. Hays said. "So interesting, your story. I do hope you can find the information you need."

"Thank you," Helen said.

Lucius followed them out of the parlor into the entrance hall, waiting for them to leave the house. What did he think they were going to do, Simon wondered, make a break for the stairs and barricade themselves in the attic?

Two children and a miniature schnauzer chasing a tennis ball barreled into the hall.

"Hey," Lucius said, "not inside! I've told you a hundred times!"

The schnauzer lost his footing on the marble floor and slid into Hays. He grabbed the dog's collar and the arm of one of the boys.

"Sorry, Dad," the boy said.

"My sons," Lucius said, introducing the boys. "Luke and Rick."

Simon saw immediately that Rick, whom he guessed was about seven, had only a quarter inch of hair on his head and dark rings under his eyes. He was painfully thin. But nonetheless, he led his brother and the dog, running, down the hall toward a back door.

"Rick has had leukemia," Lucius said, explaining his son's appearance.

"I hope he's doing well," Helen said.

"Extremely well," Lucius said. "He's had a bone marrow transplant, and the doctors tell us he's cured. We were very lucky. Several members of our family qualified as donors. That's not always the case."

"I'm so glad for you," Simon said.

Once they were in Simon's car and out of earshot, Helen exploded.

"Damn them," she said. "How could they? We were so close!"

"It's their stuff," Simon said. "They have every right to tell us we can't poke around in it."

"Do you believe the whole family lives in that house together? It's like a Gothic novel."

"Complete with skeletons in the attic," Simon said.

"I'm so frustrated! Can't we do something? Maybe Mr. Grimes could help. Do you think?"

"I don't know. I'm not sure I'd want a couple of complete strangers poking through my family history. They have to be careful, with Lucius running for the Senate. We could be Democratic moles. We did lie to them about our motives, you know."

"Don't be so rational. We could hardly tell them that I think I'm the reincarnation of their aunt's housekeeper, could we?"

"Of course not. But we have other sources to explore. Maybe Fred will remember more. He's supposed to e-mail me later this afternoon."

Simon stopped at a red light. The Thunderbird's engine idled powerfully, the radio softly played Christmas carols, and the sun glinted off the ornaments on the decorated trees in a nearby florist's window. It wasn't even noon yet. Simon realized he didn't want to take Helen back to her hotel. He tried to think of an excuse to keep her with him.

"It's not just the baby," Helen said.

"What?"

"The dead baby, that I remember burying. That's the worst memory, but you know what puzzles me almost as much? That procession of crying boys — I can visualize it so clearly — what in God's name were they doing? And did you hear Miss Henly? Annie's husband died in a fire! How did I know that? Sometimes I think I would give five years off my life to find out."

"I have an idea," Simon said. "Let's take a field trip, and we'll test another of your memories."

"Where are we going?"

"I'll tell you in a few minutes. First, go over your recollection of the cemetery and burying the baby."

"Again? Oh, why not. Let's see, it was pitch black, very late at night, and cold. Snow was deep on the ground. I couldn't see much beyond a few feet around me. I had an oil lamp with the wick turned way up and a shovel, and, I hate this, a baby in my arms. It was dead, I won't describe that again. The baby was swaddled in heavy blankets. I put her down on the snow. Then I dug a hole next to a large, square gravestone."

"It must have been difficult to dig a grave in frozen ground in the dead of winter."

"It must have been, mustn't it? But I managed. I placed the baby in the grave and covered it up, tromping the dirt down, covering the spot with brush and snow."

"Anything else?"

"No. I don't remember getting there, or leaving. Just the burial itself. It's horrible." Helen shuddered. "What if it happened? If everything else I remember is true, won't that be, too?"

"Not necessarily. I still think we'll find a reasonable explanation."

"You have to promise me something."

"What?"

"If I do turn out to be reincarnated, you won't write a book or go on television or anything."

"There's no chance of that. I'll keep it a deep secret, and start being good, so as not to come back without tenure."

Simon turned into Oakwood, the restored Victorian neighborhood in downtown Raleigh, now festive in its seasonal dress. Evergreens and red, gold, green, and silver ribbons festooned gingerbread porches. Every window glowed with an electric candle. Snow would perfect the scene, but that was unlikely as long as afternoon temperatures reached the sixties.

"These homes are lovely," Helen said. "Is this what you wanted to show me?"

"Not exactly," Simon said, turning down the street that led to Oakwood Cemetery. They drove through the iron gates. "This is where the Raleigh Christian Orphanage has its burial plot. Let's see if you recognize it."

They stopped at the cemetery office, a small stone Greek Revival building, where the cemetery manager showed them on a map where to find the Orphanage plot.

"Would you like to see the original entries?" he asked.

"Please," Simon said. "We're interested in the period between 1907, and say, 1912."

The manager drew an oversize ledger out of a file drawer. Its canvas maroon cover was faded and stained. The manager put on white cotton gloves before he opened it and turned the pages.

"There," he said, showing them handwritten entries in ink faded brown with age. "The Orphanage bought the plot in 1905. A child had died of pneumonia, and they needed somewhere to bury her."

Helen and Simon bent over the ledgers. There were just three entries for the years that interested them, all children over five years old.

"There are four marked graves and six unmarked in all," the manager said. "And the big stone, of course."

Helen and Simon thanked him, got back in Simon's car, and set off to look for the plot.

Oakwood Cemetery was a testament to Victorian funerary art. Bright white angels, crosses, towers, and mausoleums towered over more modest graves. In one corner, the stones of a regiment of Confederate soldiers stood in formation, officers arranged at the head.

"I like this place," Simon said. "I love to just walk around it, reading the markers, imagining what people's lives were like." Simon didn't mention that Anne Bloodworth was buried here. She was the heiress whose disappearance and murder in 1926 first introduced him to forensic history.

Simon pulled off onto a verge, and they both got out of the car and walked toward a large marble marker inscribed "Raleigh Christian Orphanage." Four small stones bordered the plot, the marked graves the manager had mentioned. Simon left Helen to look around, while he examined the stones. One was for a nine-year-old girl who died in the late twenties, the other three were for teenage boys. All must have had families with enough money to pay for markers.

Helen stood in front of the big gravestone, which sat squarely in the middle of the plot.

"Well?" Simon said.

"It's the right size and shape, but I don't remember seeing the inscription. And I don't recognize any of the rest of this," she said, looking around. "Could I, Annie, I mean, walk here from the Orphanage? It's a long way."

"You could have taken the trolley. Or borrowed a horse and buggy from the Orphanage."

"What about the baby?"

"If you, Annie, that is, kept her bundled up in blankets, she might have appeared to be sleeping."

Helen shrugged her shoulders in annoyance. "That's it," she said, "I can't remember another single thing."

"You're trying," Simon said. "That's all you can do."

"Sometimes I believe it, you know, that I was Annie Evans. Then all these stupid questions pop into my head. Like, where do discarnate souls live in between lives? And, since the population of the earth is increasing, where do new souls come from? And all the books and articles I've read speculate that those of us who are unfortunate enough to have these memories must have died unexpectedly, with 'unfinished business' in our past incarnation. If that's true, why can't I remember enough to take care of it?"

She leaned up against the marker, and stared out over the acres of graves.

"I don't know," Simon said. "One theory I read compares the brain to a radio receiver, and the mind to the radio station.

Minds, or souls if you prefer, live in heaven, or whatever you want to call it, and transmit to the person they inhabit at the moment. When that person dies, the receiver is gone, but that doesn't mean the radio station isn't still transmitting. It just finds a new receiver."

"That's silly. You're making fun of me."

"Sillier than heaven? Or nirvana?"

"You're not helping. I don't want to believe any of this."

"Sorry."

They went back to the car. Helen turned down Simon's invitation to lunch.

"I need to be alone for a while," she said.

Simon dropped her off at her hotel. He gave her his arm to help her climb out of the car, and felt a tingle of desire when she took it. He bit his tongue to stop himself from inviting her to go with him to Alma and Otis Gates' Christmas party that night. Best to leave social events out of their relationship, he reminded himself.

Simon found Julia's keys to his house in his mailbox when he got home. She'd come for her earrings. He was glad he'd missed her.

Simon was most of the way through a peanut butter and jelly sandwich when his doorbell rang. A tall man wearing dark slacks, a cashmere blazer, and an out-of-season tan stood on his front porch. A silver Mercedes sports car was parked on the street behind him, with the driver's door standing open and the motor idling.

"Hi," the man said, stretching out his hand to shake Simon's. "I stopped to see if I could catch you at home. I'm Jesse Lay."

"Come in," Simon said.

"Can't," Lay said. "I'm in kind of a hurry. Running late."

Simon joined him on the porch. Lay seemed anxious. He shifted his weight from foot to foot several times over the next few minutes, and alternated between smoothing his hair and jingling coins in his pockets.

"I'll get straight to the point," Lay said. "My cousin, Phoebe Hays, called me and said you wanted access to some family documents. I'd like to know what for. That genealogy thing, that's weak. I've heard of you, you're famous for solving old murders. I don't think you'd waste your time on something like that."

"I'm helping a friend."

"Whatever. Anyway, the family isn't going to grant access to someone we hardly know . . ."

"I understand."

Jesse stopped fidgeting.

"You do?"

"Of course. But I assure you we aren't looking for anything that would embarrass your family . . ."

"Whatever. The thing is, we haven't gone through that stuff ourselves. It's not organized or filed or anything. Personally I'd take it all to the landfill, it's a fire hazard, but Uncle Fred is attached to all his junk, so we have to wait until he dies. But still, we don't want somebody rummaging . . ."

"I've got it. I hear you," Simon said.

"Good," Lay said. "I've got to go."

Lay stopped halfway down the front steps.

"How well do you know my Uncle Fred?" he asked.

"I've talked to him once on the phone."

"Oh. He's old, I wouldn't trust a lot of what he says." Lay got into his car and pulled out into the street, honking to clear the intersection.

Simon closed the door behind him. This was interesting. Of course the extended Grimes family didn't want him poking around their family documents. That went without saying. Most people wouldn't. But Phoebe Hays had already refused him access, in no uncertain terms. Why had she even called Jesse, and why did he feel it necessary to come to Simon's house to emphasize their refusal? Simon wondered who owned the mansion, Fred Grimes or his daughter, and realized he'd really like to get up in that attic. Short of learning the cat burgling trade, he couldn't figure out how to do it.

Simon went upstairs to check his e-mail, taking a cold Coke with him. He logged on to his college account first, where he found a slew of messages. One reminded him of his deadlines. The week coming up was exam week; final grades were due the following Tuesday. The college president invited the faculty to the annual Christmas reception, which was the next evening. A note from the Dean of Students informed him that one of his students had a skiing accident in Asheville and was in the hospital there with a compound fracture. Of course, she'd miss his exam. Simon was sure the dean's office had verified the accident. Once he had a student who broke three bones during a single academic year, every one for real.

"Dear Professor Shaw," the final e-mail began. *"I write to you with a heavy heart. Since I'm a senior, I will likely never be able to take the one course that motivated me to attend*

Kenan College — your historiography seminar. Apparently, your office lost my registration form, and now I find myself unable to fulfill this longtime dream. If you think an extra student might fit into your classroom, or if you think you can kick someone out, please let me in. A bright light will open upon my spirit.

Peace, Kevin Pratt."

Simon counted to ten before hitting the reply button.

"Dear Kevin," he responded. *"I'll add your name to the waiting list for this seminar. Peace to you, too. — Prof. Shaw."*

Simon printed out Kevin's plea and put it in his briefcase to add to the growing file of appeals in his office.

Simon logged on to his personal e-mail account where he found a long message from his uncle, Morris Simon. Morris vented at length on the tense political situation in the Middle East, his daughter Leah's insistence on attending graduate school in meteorology instead of working in the family business (you go, girl!), and his son Seth's regrettable choice of a career in public health over a more profitable medical specialty. He attached some photographs of the Wailing Wall surrounded by drifting snow from a freak blizzard that had struck Israel. Then he reminded Simon that he could still change his mind and come to New York for his winter holidays. Simon felt a pang of loneliness. Suddenly, he wanted to be there, sleeping on the sofa in the den of their overheated apartment, going to temple with his uncle, overfed by his aunt. He wanted to escort Leah, his favorite relative, to an expensive dinner and the opera. Why didn't he just go? He could jump on a plane right after Christmas dinner at Marcus' home.

He almost replied affirmatively, then recollected Helen Williams. He didn't know how long it would be until there was resolution to her case, and he couldn't abandon her. He didn't want to leave Raleigh until he'd done all he could for her. Instead he e-mailed his uncle that he couldn't change his plans, but that he'd visit over spring break for sure, if that was okay.

A long e-mail from Fred Grimes followed.

"Dear Simon," he wrote. *"What did I tell you? I knew I would remember more. What's annoying is, I forgot such an obvious person for you to interview. John Malone worked as a driver for Stella and her family for years. He's a few years younger than me. He left the Orphanage in 1940, but a bad leg kept him out of the military. He knew Miss Annie as a boy, of*

course, and then when he worked for Stella. After Stella died, he worked for her son Joe and his wife. He's retired now, but he lives in an apartment over the garage at Phoebe's and watches the house when no one is home. Keeping my pen and paper handy to record more memory spurts, your friend, Fred Grimes."

Simon turned off his computer. A direct link to Annie Evans lived right there at the Hays house and Phoebe Hays not only didn't mention him, she denied knowing anyone at all who worked for Stella. Why would she do that? What did she think Malone might tell them?

Simon swiveled in his chair, looked up Malone's phone number, and called him. He got no answer or voice mail. Then he flipped through the phone book, finding a listing for the Raleigh Christian Foundation. It was Saturday, but a secretary was in the office finishing up an agenda for Monday's meeting of the Board of Directors. It took Simon just a few minutes to learn that the Foundation was formed with the money from the sale of the Orphanage property; its mission was to fund children's services. Phoebe Hays was on the Board of Directors, "inheriting" the position from her father, who had assumed it after his sister Stella died. The Foundation had the Orphanage archives in storage. Simon would need the permission of the Board of Directors to examine them. The secretary suggested he call back first thing Monday morning and ask the staff to take his request for access to the board that day.

7

> People like us, who believe in physics, know that the distinction between past, present, and future is only a stubbornly persistent illusion.
>
> — ALBERT EINSTEIN

Simon reached Fred Grimes later in the afternoon, after Fred returned from his water aerobics class.

"It's the only exercise I can do at my age," Fred said.

Simon inquired about the Grimes family's involvement in the Raleigh Christian Foundation.

"You know how these things work," Fred said. "Stella was a wealthy alumna of the Orphanage, so naturally she was asked to serve on the Board of Directors after the Orphanage property was sold, and after she died, I was invited to replace her. Phoebe inherited my seat after I retired, and Lucius was the treasurer for a number of years. All we did was convene once a year, stuff ourselves with gourmet refreshments, then vote to grant money to the projects the staff recommended."

Simon mentioned that he was going to ask the board's permission to look through the Orphanage archives.

"I'll talk to Phoebe and tell her I expect her to vote to approve your request," Fred said. "Have you talked to John Malone yet?"

"Haven't reached him," Simon said.

"He'll be able to tell you something about Annie," Fred said. "And there's something else niggling at the edge of my mind. I just can't bring it up. I'll remember eventually."

"I don't suppose you'd allow me to go into your attic and go through your stuff looking for information about Annie, would you?"

"Sure. Wouldn't bother me any."

"Your daughter and grandson said no. I think Lucius is worried I might turn up some dirty linen and wave it around during his election campaign."

"Like I said, it's fine with me, but if Phoebe and Lucius think it might hurt his career, my chances of getting them to change their minds are zero and nil. Sorry."

While waiting to call John Malone again, Simon caught up on his notes. Reviewing them was embarrassing. He would burn them when he was finished with this case. If anyone other than his closest friends found out he was investigating a past-life regression, well, the consequences didn't bear thinking about.

When he was with Helen, their quest seemed natural and reasonable. She was intelligent and funny, and very attractive, he thought, remembering the twinge of lust he'd suffered when handing her out of his car.

When she wasn't around, his common sense prevailed, and he was forced to question her mental health. She had to have psychological problems. Could she be so disturbed that she wasn't even aware that she had concocted this outlandish story? If she had invented it deliberately, what could be her motive? He saw no sign that she intended to capitalize on whatever they learned about Annie Evans. In fact, Helen seemed eager to keep her search secret.

He firmly reminded himself that he was a scholar, and that he was obliged to investigate Helen's claims objectively. This meant that he had to accept the possibility of two distasteful solutions, the first, that Helen was mentally ill and had made up the entire story after studying the early history of the

Orphanage herself, and the second, that she was recalling an actual past incarnation. He'd prefer that the answer lay somewhere between those two extremes, but he couldn't alter the truth to suit himself, no matter how unpleasant or unlikely it might seem.

Miss Henly made it clear that she was disgusted with him. Simon could sense the disapproval in her voice over the telephone line.

"Just what do you mean, Professor Shaw?" she asked him. "Checking up on that nice young woman."

"I have to ask," Simon said, "if you'd talked to her before our visit this morning?"

"Of course not. What are you implying?"

"Nothing," Simon said. "Nothing at all."

"I certainly hope not," she said.

John Malone answered the telephone on the second ring.

"I took my wife to the train station," he said. "She's visiting our daughter in Charlotte."

He listened while Simon explained his interest in Annie Evans and Stella Grimes Lay, and what he had already learned.

"I'll bet," Malone said, "that Frank and

Nancy Webb told you a lot of mushy stories about how wonderful life at the Orphanage was, how we were all like brothers and sisters, and how much better off we were there than out in the cold, cruel world."

"You don't buy into that?" Simon asked.

"Hell, no. I despised it there. I ran away three times, but my daddy kept making me go back. I finally gave up and counted the days until I graduated."

"Could I come over and ask you some questions?"

"Sure, why not? Don't drive in the front, though. Come in the back way and park behind the garage. I'm the help. My visitors are supposed to use the service alley."

Simon did as he was instructed, parking behind the Hays' four-car garage. The back of the mansion faced him as he walked around the garage to the stairway that led up to Malone's upstairs apartment. A long wing, Lucius' residence, he supposed, extended off the far end of the house and partly enclosed a formal garden. The rear windows of the main house, bare of Christmas decorations, looked blankly out over a glassed-in conservatory and a slate patio, its furniture shrouded with covers for the winter.

At the top of the steep stairs, John Malone

opened his door. He was in his late eighties — bald, with just a wisp of gray hair straying over his ears, and faded brown eyes. A blue cardigan missing a button hung from his stooped shoulders. He had a television remote control in one hand and a striped jelly glass full of iced gold liquid in the other.

Malone limped as he led Simon into his cluttered living room, where the remains of a take-out barbecue plate littered the coffee table. He muted the basketball game playing on the console television.

"My wife won't let me eat or drink nothing I like anymore," Malone said. "So after I dropped her off at the Amtrak, I made a beeline to the liquor store and then to Cooper's Bar-B-Q. She'll be gone for a couple of days, and I'm going to enjoy myself. I'm going to watch ESPN, and drink bourbon and ginger ale, and eat barbecue and banana puddin' all day long."

Malone eased himself into a well-worn recliner and motioned for Simon to sit on the sofa.

"So," he said, "what do you want to know?"

"Tell me about Annie Evans."

"She was like all the matrons at the Orphanage. She was a widow who had to support herself somehow, so she took care of unwanted children. Those days, there wasn't much else she could do. She couldn't type, and she couldn't afford to set herself up as a telephone operator, and she wasn't good-looking enough to get a job in a store."

"That's a cynical view."

Malone shrugged. "Maybe. Do you know why the Orphanage was founded? Not to feed and clothe us, not for charity's sake, but to keep the boys out of prison and the girls off the street. To protect virtuous churchgoers, folks who had homes and jobs, from the riffraff. It says so right in the charter. My daddy sent me there after Momma took off. He didn't want to fool with me."

Malone finished his drink and poured a new one. "Want one?" he said, tilting the Old Granddad bourbon bottle toward Simon.

"No thanks."

"We worked like dogs. The girls did all the cooking and cleaning, washing and ironing. The boys chopped wood, grew vegetables, and milked cows at the dairy. A couple times a year, we went down to the train station and unloaded a railroad car full of coal into wagons, drove them back to the

Orphanage, and shoveled the coal into all the boiler rooms. We were black as coal ourselves when we were done. The Orphanage owned Oberlin Farm, when Oberlin Road was still out in the country. We raised and butchered a hundred hogs there every year, and we sugared and smoked the meat ourselves. You know what happened to the hams? The superintendent gave them to the Orphanage patrons. The orphans got the side meat. I got even, though. Every year I stole some of those hams and sold them. Spent the money on Luckies, Pepsi-Colas, and candy down at the grocery store on Devereux Street."

Malone stretched his bum leg out in front of him, wincing a bit as he flexed it.

"Then there was the church. We went to church three damn times a week, Wednesday evening, Sunday morning, and Sunday evening. When we weren't in church, someone was reading to us from the Bible, night and day, it seemed like. And a dozen times a year, we'd get dressed up and go sing hymns to some church women's group somewhere, like trained monkeys, so they'd give the Orphanage money. It's funny, though, you know what my wife says?"

"What?"

"She says the Orphanage won. I graduated high school, got married, stayed married, worked hard all my life, and went to church most Sundays and put money in the collection plate. I go to the Orphanage alumni reunion every Easter. I turned out just the way they wanted me to."

Then a broad smile creased his face.

"But you don't want to know about my miserable childhood, you want to know about Annie Evans," he said. "I never was at the Baby Cottage. When I got to the Orphanage, I lived straight off in the boys' dormitory. That was after the two weeks every kid was quarantined in the infirmary, so you didn't pass on measles, mumps, or tuberculosis to the rest of the kids.

"Miss Annie was real nice, though she was quieter than the other matrons. When I graduated, this was after she'd left to work for Stella herself, she recommended me to Stella and her husband. They wanted a driver, and since my leg kept me from going to the War like most of the boys did my year, I was glad to have the job. So I drove their car, serviced it, and did errands and chores. Over the years, I polished enough silver to fill Fort Knox. I bartended at all their parties. After Stella died, I worked for her son Joe and his wife until they died in a car accident. It was my day off, and Joe was driving. After Joe died, I came to work for Fred's family. Jesse and I never got along. He wasn't half the man his father was."

"When did Annie die?"

"In the late fifties, I think. Maybe a little later. She was old enough by then that she wasn't working anymore. They'd put her out to pasture, let her live at the family's summer place, like I do here. She liked it out there. Said the country reminded her of her childhood."

"You don't remember the exact date she died, do you? Even the year would be helpful."

"No. I had driven Stella and her husband to Norfolk, to catch the boat to England. I don't remember the year. They went abroad almost every year. Mr. Fred sent them a telegram about her death. I didn't get back in time for the funeral. I hate funerals. I'm not going to have one, myself."

Simon could hardly go to the state records office and look through all the deaths in Wake County in the late fifties. Someone had to remember something specific about this woman so he could track her down.

"Do you know where she's buried?" he asked Malone. Annie's birth and death dates would be engraved on her tombstone.

"No," said Malone. "Not a clue. Definitely not in the Grimes' plot. I been there."

"Do you know Annie's maiden name? Where she lived before she went to the Orphanage? Her birthday?"

Malone frowned, his brows creasing in deep furrows.

"No," he said. "Sorry. She never talked about herself. She was devoted to Stella and Joe, and Jesse, too, though he was a little boy when she died."

Simon told the old man about his visit to the Orphanage's plot in Oakwood Cemetery. He mentioned the four marked graves.

"I knew one of those boys," he said. "Cliff Wallace was his name. He was beaten to death by the football coach."

Simon was shocked. "What did you say?" he asked.

"He was beaten to death. Oh, it was hushed up. High school football was so important back then, and the Orphanage's team was real good. But Cliff had messed up a couple of plays, so we didn't get to the state finals. The coach was furious, and got plastered on home-brewed beer. He wanted to move on to coach one of the big high schools, you see. Anyway, while he was drunk, he beat the stuffing out of Cliff. Kid died of pneumonia a week later. The Orphanage hushed it up, said it was unrelated to the beating. Of course it was the broken ribs that started the pneumonia."

"What an awful thing."

"Annie Evans was one of the matrons that raised hell about it. Coach was fired. He should have gone to jail."

"Were beatings unusual?"

"A bad one, yeah. The male staff whipped the boys sometimes. The worst were the boys themselves. The big boys beat the little boys, then the little boys grew up to be big boys. It was a vicious circle. I have to be fair to the staff and say we didn't tell on each other. It was rough. I'll never forget my first bug funeral."

"What's a bug funeral?"

Malone sighed. "What would happen," he said, "was, some of the big boys would kill a bug and put it in a matchbox. Then we'd have a funeral for it. The big boys would beat up the little ones so we'd be crying hard, like mourners, and we'd all march around the grounds. Then we'd stop under a tree, bury the matchbox, and one of the boys would preach the funeral service. If we weren't crying hard enough, they'd hit us again. We used slivers of acorn and such for the host, and drank water out of acorn caps for the wine. The superintendent and staff hated bug funerals because we were making fun of religion. But we did it anyway."

Jesse Lay's Mercedes was parked behind the garage next to Simon's Thunderbird, but Jesse was nowhere in sight. Phoebe leaned against Simon's car, obviously waiting for him. She glanced at her watch just before Simon walked up to her.

"You must think terribly of me," she said.

"No," Simon said, "not at all."

"I don't want you to think that I didn't mention John Malone to you intentionally. It just slipped my mind, that's all. He's been with the family so long, I didn't remember that he'd come from the Orphanage until after you left."

"That's okay."

"Was he able to help you?"

"Some. By the way, I talked to your father today, and he said he had no objection to me going through any documents he stored in your attic, if you agreed."

Phoebe had added a blue raw silk blazer to her ensemble and she carried a briefcase-size leather purse. She edged along the car toward the back entrance to the garage, eager to get away.

"I'm sorry," she said. "I just can't do that.

But let's compromise. After the election it would be okay — that's not unreasonable, is it?"

"No," Simon said, "it's not, but the election is months away. My friend is anxious to know if Annie Evans is related to her."

"I don't know why. The woman's been dead for years. What can she matter to anyone now?"

Simon shrugged, so frustrated by now he didn't bother to answer. If the woman didn't understand that everyone's life mattered, no matter how long ago they lived, that unheralded individuals could change the course of history, that Annie's life and death influenced Phoebe's own family's history, then he didn't have the energy to waste explaining it to her.

On the drive home, Simon worried about Helen, specifically whether or not he should tell her about the bug funeral. In the end he decided against it. He was concerned that any more revelations that her memories were accurate, without an explanation of their origin, might cause her great anguish. Of course, he was obliged to tell her eventually, whether he was able to help her solve her problem or not.

Wearing his Christmas party best, a black

leather jacket and a green tie emblazoned with tiny Santas, Simon drove into southeast Raleigh, heading for Otis and Alma Gates' annual holiday open house.

Simon had met Detective Sergeant Otis Gates several years ago, when Anne Bloodworth's corpse was unearthed on the grounds of Kenan College. The two men worked together to solve her murder, and Otis introduced Simon to Julia. Simon and Otis became good friends despite their differences; Simon was small, white, and liberal, while Otis was big, African-American, and conservative. Their friendship easily survived Simon's breakup with Julia.

Otis had met his wife Alma twenty-some-odd years ago at an Aretha Franklin concert. They now had two teenage sons, Joshua and Eli, just eighteen months apart. Joshua was the older, a senior in high school, an overachiever with full scholarships in engineering to three colleges. Eli, a big man like his father, lived for the saxophone. "Thank God he's got to keep a two-point-oh to travel with the high school band," Otis said. "Otherwise he'd never crack a book. Joshua, now, I have to remind him to lighten up."

Alma Gates was the music director at the Jubilee AME (African Methodist Episcopal) Church. She sang like an angel. Hearing her belt out "Amazing Grace" could bring tears to your eyes.

It was Eli who stood in front of the Gates' home, directing traffic to various parking areas around the neighborhood.

"Hey, Dr. Shaw, Merry Christmas," the tall teenager said, leaning into Simon's car window.

"Merry Christmas to you, too, Eli," Simon said.

"Go on down there," Eli said, pointing, "about a block. See the entrance to the playground? There're still some spaces there, I think."

Cars jammed the street, most parked with a couple of wheels up on the sidewalk. Sure enough, there were spaces left at the playground. Simon parked, then strolled back to Otis' house. As he headed down the street, he thought about what he always did when he visited Otis' house. Why was it, after all these years of struggle, neighborhoods were still segregated? Simon's ex-hippie, liberal neighborhood was lily-white. Otis' solidly middle-class subdivision in southeast Raleigh was exclusively African-American. He and Otis had discussed this. "What you all want," Otis would say, "is for a couple of nice, harmless, well-off black families, preferably without male teenagers who like rap music, to move in so you can casserole them to death. I don't feel obliged to live my life so you can feel good about yourselves. I just want to be comfortable in my own skin, so to speak, and I want my boys to be comfortable in theirs."

Otis opened the door.

"Hey, there," Simon said, "I'm just here for the food."

"We've got a few trays of stale crackers and moldy cheese left," Otis said, "and no, Julia's not here."

Simon was relieved, and caught himself wishing he'd invited Helen along.

He pushed himself through the throng of guests. The motley group included uniformed police officers snatching a few minutes from their shifts, a couple of scruffy young men whom Simon thought must be undercover agents, teenaged friends of the Gates boys, neighbors, and Alma's fellow choir members, already dressed in their sky blue robes, ready for their role in a Christmas nativity drama at the church later that night.

Simon paused in the doorway of the dining room. Caribbean delicacies, cooked from scratch from recipes inherited from Alma's Jamaican grandmother, covered the dining table. People three deep ringed the table, reaching over each other for chicken curry, rice and peas, and banana fritters. On a sideboard stood a frosty bowl of eggnog speckled with nutmeg, and a Crock-Pot steaming with hot apple cider and cinnamon sticks.

Simon spotted his friend David Morgan through the French doors into the sunroom. He joined him there. Morgan wore his usual flannel shirt, corduroys, and work boots, dressed up with a khaki travel blazer in honor of the occasion. His beard was neatly trimmed. A modest beer belly hung over his belt. They exchanged Christmas greetings.

"Listen," Morgan said, leaning toward Simon and half-whispering, "I can't find the booze. Do they have it in another room?"

"Alma doesn't drink, and she disapproves of anyone else drinking. The Jamaican fruitcake is soaked in rum, but that's all the alcohol you'll get in this house."

Morgan looked as surprised as if he'd been told the Gates didn't heat their house in winter.

"But Otis drinks."

"Not at home, he doesn't," Simon said. The two men cleaned their plates down to the last crumb while they watched a frustrated squirrel test a squirrel-proof bird feeder in the Gates' backyard. When they were finished, they took their plates into the kitchen. Alma was there, arranging ham biscuits on a platter. She hugged Simon's neck and he kissed her cheek.

"Don't leave before I bring out the fruitcake," she said.

"Not a chance," Simon said, slipping a biscuit off the tray before she got out of the kitchen.

"Let's go mingle for a while," Simon said to Morgan. "Then after we have our cake, we can go out for a drink." An hour and a half later, after two slices of cake and an impromptu rendition of "Oh, Holy Night" by Alma and her choir, the two men left and drove in their respective cars to the Draft House in Cameron Village, where they ordered a pitcher of the best beer in the place.

While they drank, they talked about holiday plans, ACC basketball, Morgan's latest excavation, and Simon's book on the coastal history of North Carolina, of which he had written exactly seven pages.

"I'll be retired before it's published," Simon said. He wasn't really complaining. He preferred to teach, anyway. He stayed at Kenan because the school emphasized teaching over publication.

They avoided the subject of women.

Simon wasn't in the mood to whine about his love life. Morgan, after years of confirmed bachelorhood, was dating a lady Episcopal priest from Durham. Simon was curious about the relationship, but figured Morgan would talk about it if he wanted to.

Well into their second beer, Simon brought up the existential.

"Tell me," he said, "do you believe in an afterlife?"

"Jesus," Morgan said, "what brought that on?" He drank the rest of his glass of beer, wiped foam off his beard, and poured himself another. "To answer you, no, definitely not."

"What do you believe in?"

"Science. I believe in science."

"That's all?"

"That's enough. What can be observed, that's what I believe in."

"That's excludes a lot of thought and philosophy, not to mention love."

"Human beings have a very rich imagination."

"Albert Einstein believed in God."

"The brain," Morgan said, scratching out a crude illustration on a napkin, "is complicated, to say the least. But we know some things about it. Here is Broca's spot, for example, where speech resides. It's very poorly developed in apes, and even in homo erectus. Here is the area which processes evidence. And here is the place belief inhabits, we think." He put down his pencil and drank a couple inches of beer.

"So?" Simon said.

"So belief exists separately from reality. Humans believe what they need to believe. This is why people believe weird things — like reincarnation or heaven or alien abductions, even though they're rational in other areas of their lives. Concepts of the afterlife arose when human animals evolved enough to realize they were going to die."

"Ouch."

"You don't agree with me."

"No, I don't." Simon wondered, but didn't ask, if Morgan had discussed any of this with his woman friend, the priest.

"I'm not surprised. You're a social scientist."

The two men finished the pitcher of beer.

"Want another?" Morgan asked.

"No," Simon said. "I want to test a hypothesis. Scientifically, that is."

"I'm game. What's the hypothesis?"

"Is your archaeology stuff in your truck?"

"Yeah. What are we digging up?"

They left the Thunderbird in Simon's

driveway and drove off in Morgan's truck. Simon's sleek car was too conspicuous for prowling around Raleigh at night.

"If I hadn't had a couple of beers, you couldn't get me to do this," Morgan said. "Where exactly are we going, anyway?"

"If I told you, you wouldn't go. Just head toward Oakwood, okay?" Simon said.

They drove into the quiet Victorian neighborhood Simon and Helen had visited that afternoon. A few homeowners on the street had forgotten to turn off their Christmas lights. One set, directly opposite the Oakwood Cemetery, blinked randomly, first red, then green, then white.

Simon directed Morgan to park his truck a couple of blocks away, and the two men walked to the small cemetery side entrance Simon had noticed earlier in the day. The narrow wrought-iron gate hung between two brick and concrete pillars on the corner of Oakwood Avenue and Person Street.

Morgan carried his surplus military duffel bag containing the tools of his trade; shovels, brushes, dental picks, and such. When they reached the cemetery gate, he stopped.

"We're not," he said.

"Yes, we are," Simon said.

"We're breaking into Oakwood Cemetery? What are you planning to do, rob graves?"

"Look," Simon said. "Trust me. I need your expertise. Besides, we're not going to find anything."

"If we get caught . . ."

"We won't. It's two o'clock in the morning. And there's no night watchman."

"You sure?"

"Yeah. I called and checked."

Simon scrambled easily over the top of the gate and dropped onto grass on the other side. Morgan hesitated.

"I think I'll go over the wall," he said, whispering. "It's not as high."

"I wouldn't. There's razor wire along the top," Simon said.

Morgan tossed his tool bag over the fence. Simon caught it, and laid it on the ground. He raised his arms, as if to catch his friend should he fall.

"Get out of the way," Morgan said. "You don't want me to crush you."

Grumbling, Morgan hoisted his bulk over the gate, and dropped to the other side, slipping and falling onto the satchel of tools. The noise made them both drop flat to the ground and listen.

There was no sound from the nearby houses.

"You're positive there's no night watchman?" Morgan asked.

"You don't think I'd be doing this if I thought there was any chance of getting caught, do you?"

The two men got to their feet.

"It's over here," Simon said. He clicked on a flashlight, cupping it in both hands to reduce the amount of light it shed. The two men crept softly down a well-groomed path lined with gravestones. All that white marble glowed in the moonshine, casting deep shadows between the graves, adding to the macabre atmosphere of the cemetery. Many of the monuments were wondrous and huge, angels soaring into heaven, or crosses reminding one of the promises of resurrection, and some were tiny cubes, barely more than rocks, with one initial carved into them. They passed a fresh grave, with a tent still raised over it and bunches of dying flowers spread over the mound of red Carolina clay.

"Spooky," Simon said.

"The only thing I'm scared of is getting arrested," Morgan said. "Let's do this and get out of here."

Simon's beer-induced bravado was waning, and he almost suggested that they abandon their mission and go home. But he knew there was only one way to test Helen's story. He was eager to get it over with.

"Here we are," Simon said, stopping at the Raleigh Christian Orphanage plot.

Morgan read the inscriptions on the small stones, calculating the ages of the children buried there. "Fourteen years old," he said. "Sixteen. Eleven. Six. Poor little guys. In over a hundred years, just four kids died?"

"There are a half-dozen more, unmarked. I checked the register in the office this afternoon."

"Now that I'm sober, please explain what we're doing here," Morgan said.

Simon chose his words carefully. He wanted to give away as little as possible, even to his closest friend.

"I have reason to think that a child was buried here secretly, many years ago. The grave isn't marked, but I know where it's supposed to be. I want to find out if this is true. My source told me where the body should be — over there," Simon said, indicating a spot next to the large gravestone.

"Isn't there some other way for you to find out?" Morgan asked. "Instead of us coming out here in the middle of the night?"

"I can't betray a confidence."

"We're going to put everything back the way it was?"

"Absolutely."

"And you don't expect to find a body?"

"Of course not. I'm trying to put a person's mind at rest. It seems the only way I can do that is to dig in this spot and prove to her there's no corpse there."

"Okay."

The two men stood quietly for a minute, listening. There was no sound.

With an instant camera from Morgan's tool bag Simon snapped a photograph of the spot next to the large gravestone where he intended to dig. He signed the picture, inscribing the time, and handed it to Morgan, who signed it also. Then Simon got down on his knees and, using his pocket knife, cut a large rectangle into the turf. The dead grass was tangled into a dense mat, and he was able to tug the rectangle of sod out of the ground and set it aside, so that later he could replace it.

"Okay," he said, standing up and wiping his hands on his jeans. "Let's do it."

Morgan shoveled until the depth of the hole was about a foot, then Simon relieved him. Another foot, and the shovel struck something. The sound was a creepy soft thunk, and both men froze.

"Let me finish this," Morgan said, removing a trowel from his duffel.

Please let this be a tree root, Simon said to himself.

"I see cloth," Morgan said. He looked up at his friend. Simon was silent, his mouth pressed in a thin line, forehead furrowed.

Simon got down on his knees next to Morgan, propping the flashlight on the big stone so that they could see into the hole.

Simon watched as Morgan carefully exposed a bundle of decaying rags. With a trowel he carefully eased aside the layers.

"Jesus," Morgan said. "It's a baby." He stopped and sat back on his haunches, dropping his trowel to the ground. "You said we weren't going to find anything."

"I know. I didn't expect this. Not at all."

Simon was appalled at the enormity of what the two of them had done. His only consolation was that he was completely surprised. So much for not having to cope with a corpse on this case.

Without saying another word, Simon took several photographs of the tiny skeleton, dressed in what was left of a long lace garment and matching cap. From the size of the corpse, he guessed the child was about a year and a half old. The muscles in his neck and scalp began to winch a band of pain around his head.

"Now we call the police, right?" Morgan said.

"We can't," Simon said.

"We have to," Morgan said. "There's this law called the Unmarked Human Burial and Human Skeletal Remains Protection Act. We have to call the police and the medical examiner."

"Not right now. I need more time to sort this out."

"This little escapade of yours could escalate quickly into a crime."

"It won't. I'll find a way to notify the authorities about the body without compromising my source, or involving the two of us."

"I don't believe this. Simon, this is extremely serious."

"I'll build a fire wall. I'll think of a way to lead the police here without telling them about tonight. I'll keep you out of it."

"This is against my better judgment," Morgan said. "I could lose my job. I might never work in archaeology again."

"I promise. No one will know you were here. No matter what happens."

"Let's get the hell away. We'll talk about it later."

Quickly they packed earth down on the

tiny body, tamping it gently every few inches as they replaced it. Simon returfed the area with the rectangle of dirt and grass he had removed. He smoothed the seams together as best he could.

"That won't pass close inspection," Morgan said.

"It doesn't have to," Simon said. "No one comes here."

The two men left the cemetery just as they came, careful not to make any noise. No one saw or heard them. Back in Morgan's truck, they both exhaled in relief.

"You said we wouldn't find a body," Morgan said again.

"I know." Simon looked at his instant photographs, one at a time, as if to remind himself of their gruesome discovery.

"I've got to have a cigarette," Morgan said.

He lit up and dangled his smoke out the truck window. A tasteful, wooden Santa, looking like an oversize garden gnome, stared at him from the closest yard.

Then they drove store back to Simon's house, passing the Krispy Kreme donut store on Person Street. It was closed, the "hot" sign, sadly, dark. Simon wanted a donut as badly as Morgan craved his nicotine.

"I need your professional opinion," Simon said to his friend. "When do you think that baby's corpse was buried? Could it have been uncovered recently, or even buried recently?"

Morgan started shaking his head before Simon had even finished his question.

"That child was interred a century ago, I estimate, and hasn't been disturbed since."

"Nineteen ten," Simon said. "It was buried in nineteen ten."

"Who told you about this? Tell me that, at least."

"The person who buried the baby. It's a girl, by the way."

"That's impossible," Morgan said. "Whoever buried the child is dead. Unless your source is the oldest person in North Carolina."

"She's twenty-eight," Simon said. He told Morgan the whole story.

Morgan lit another cigarette.

"I can't think of anything sensible to say, except there must be a reasonable explanation."

"Of course," Simon said. "But I haven't found it yet."

"Do I detect romantic involvement with this woman?"

"No."

"Good. Because I suspect she's sick."

Simon didn't argue with him. If he were Morgan, he'd feel the same way.

Morgan stopped his truck in front of Simon's house.

"I leave for my sister's in Tennessee tomorrow," he said, "which is a good thing, since there'll soon be a North Carolina warrant out for my arrest."

"I said I'd take care of it, and I will," Simon said.

Simon went inside his house, upstairs, and straight for his medicine chest. By now the vise that circled his head was ratcheted so tight his eyes felt like they might pop out of their sockets. He dosed himself with sumatriptan and codeine and filled an ice-pack, positioning the cold against his throbbing head. He curled up in a fetal position in his bed until the pounding dissipated and he fell asleep.

Simon woke up late Sunday morning. His headache was gone, and he unfolded his body, stretched, then waited for the energy to get up. He was terribly tired. He finally rose, pulled on a bathrobe, and went downstairs, where he found the instant photographs of the baby's grave on a table where he'd tossed them when he'd gotten home. What now? He'd promised Morgan he'd somehow pass the knowledge of the corpse along to the authorities without telling them what the two men had done. Exactly how was he going to do that? An anonymous phone call? Once the police verified the body existed, they wouldn't twiddle their thumbs, they'd start looking for the caller. And what was he going to say to Helen? To think he had been anxious about the consequences of telling her about the bug funeral.

He went into his kitchen and brewed some coffee. He fed his cats, toasted an English muffin and ate it, heaped with peach jam, at his kitchen table. After two cups of coffee, he felt a little better. Morgan would be in Tennessee for a week, which gave him time to think. He wouldn't tell Helen about the corpse right now. If she took it badly, he wouldn't know what to do.

Morgan was undoubtedly right that the grave was as old as Helen said it was, and that it had never been disturbed. It was his job to know such things. So how did Helen know the baby's corpse was there? Had she heard it from someone, some witness to the event that she didn't remember? Or, had she been there, and buried the child herself, when she lived as Annie Evans? He was just about ready to believe it. He no longer cared what anybody said about brain structure and evidence and religion or anything else.

When he picked up his telephone, the beeping signaled him that he had a message. He winced when he heard Helen's voice. He deleted her message without listening to all of it. He just could not deal with her. He'd call her later.

Simon showered and dressed, then attempted to read the Sunday newspaper. He read the same article three times without remembering any of it. He didn't laugh at a single comic strip, not even *Non Sequitur* or *Boondocks*. He'd already checked his e-mail, and he had nothing from Fred Grimes. It was only one o'clock in the afternoon. His exams were written and term papers graded. He would lose his mind if he couldn't find something to do.

He remembered telling Helen yesterday, which seemed years ago, that Annie Evans could have gotten to the graveyard from the Orphanage on the trolley. Could she have? It would be interesting to know, and it would take him a good part of the afternoon to find out.

He showered and dressed, filled his pockets with dimes he kept on hand for the copy machines, stuffed his notebook in his jacket, and went to that storehouse of information, the cradle of civilization and watchdog of democracy, the free public library.

The local history library was on the grounds of the Wake County Office Park. It was named after Olivia Raney, Raleigh's first librarian, whom might have known Annie, Simon mused, if Annie had possessed a library card.

After greeting the librarian, who fortunately didn't recognize him — Simon wasn't in the mood for the pleasantries required of local celebrities — he located the microfilm files. He urgently wanted a detailed map of the Orphanage and its neighborhood in 1910, and he knew where to find one.

Next to infectious disease, fire was feared most by people of the early twentieth century. They lived daily with the open flames of candles, fireplaces, parlor stoves, gas and oil lamps, and hot kitchen ranges. Homeowners and businessmen with a few extra pennies purchased fire insurance for their property. To help insurance agencies determine risk, the Sanborn Map Company of Pelham, New York, produced thousands of detailed maps of American cities, each showing the size, shape, and construction of dwellings, commercial buildings, and factories as well as fire walls, locations of windows and doors, sprinkler systems, and types of roofs. The maps also indicated widths and names of streets, property boundaries, building use, and house and block numbers.

Simon quickly located the 1910 Sanborn Fire Insurance map of Raleigh. Scrolling from page to page, he found the Orphanage. Every building on the property was clearly rendered — the girls' and boys' dormitories, the infirmary, the administration building, and the school. Other pages depicted the streets and houses that bordered the Orphanage property. The tiny neighborhood south of the Orphanage was called Brooklyn, interestingly enough, after one of the streets that ran through it. Using his dime collection, Simon photocopied half a dozen maps off the microfilm reader. After borrowing scissors and tape from the librarian, he cut and fit together the bits he wanted until he had a detailed map of the Orphanage and the Brooklyn neighborhood. It was difficult to read the tiny markings, but the first thing he noticed was that Annie Evans could have ridden the trolley down Glenwood Avenue, changed cars at the intersection with Peace Street, and ridden all the way to the cemetery. If the trolley didn't run at night, she could have borrowed a horse and buggy from the Orphanage farm. She had been a farmer's wife; she would certainly have known how to harness up the horse and drive the buggy.

He spent the next hour carefully filling in the names of the residents of each house by matching the street numbers on the maps with addresses in the 1910 city directory.

Simon called Helen on the cell phone from his car, steeling himself to speak calmly, as if he hadn't found a century-old child's corpse the night before.

"Want to go on another field trip?" he asked her.

"Sure. Can I ask where to?"

"Nineteen-ten."

8

As the soul, wearing this material body, experiences the stages of infancy, youth, manhood, and old age, even so shall it, in due time, pass on to another body, and in other incarnations shall it live again, and move and play its part.

— *BHAGAVAD-GITA*

Simon picked Helen up outside her motel. She climbed into the low T-bird, sliding in hips first. She wore a turquoise cable-knit sweater, scoop-necked, that just grazed her cleavage, and snug jeans. Simon liked a woman with curves, and Helen had them. Despite the horrors of the night before and his concerns about her mental stability, he was glad to see her, pleased to be spending an afternoon with her.

"This doesn't involve time travel, or a séance, or anything, does it?" she asked, slamming the door of the T-bird. "If it does, I don't have the strength."

"Just checking out your old neighborhood."

"Okay, then."

Within a few minutes, Simon pulled into the parking lot at the Brevard House, where Helen had fainted a couple of days ago. The two of them got out of the car and stepped up onto its creaky porch. Simon tried the door, which was, as he expected, locked. The two of them peered through the wavy glass of a front window. The interior of the house had been restored, the walls papered with reproduction paisley Victorian wallpaper, the woodwork painted in coordinating dark colors. A heavy staircase led from the entrance hall upstairs.

"The children used to line up on those stairs, in their nightclothes, one per step, so I could give them each a tablespoon of cod liver oil," Helen said. "I used the same spoon for all of them. . . ." She clapped her hand over her mouth. "Oh, my God!"

"Is that a new memory?"

"Yes! Yes, it is! I don't believe it! I remembered more!"

She hopped up and down in her excitement, seizing his hand. "Where do we go next? Come on!"

She dragged Simon off the porch in her hurry. He consulted his map and turned to his left, pointing.

"You would have walked this way many

times, if you were really Annie Evans," he said. "Let's see what you remember."

"Oh, I get it, Professor," she said. "It's a test. What do I get if I pass?"

"If your life is like mine, another test."

This time Simon took her hand, guiding her toward Clay Street, but he didn't let go of it when they got there.

"Where was I going when I walked down this street?" she asked.

"See if you remember."

Surprisingly little had changed in the tiny neighborhood since the early 1900s. The small houses, originally built for draymen, bakers, and other working-class men and their families, had been bought and restored by teachers, artisans, musicians, and others who couldn't afford to live in nearby up-scale neighborhoods.

Simon and Helen ambled down the dogleg that was Clay Street, without a flicker of recognition from Helen. When they turned left onto Brooklyn, Simon felt her hesitate. She stopped in front of a single-story bungalow painted baby-chick yellow, with bright white trim around the porch and the two front windows and a raspberry pink front door. Icicle lights, barely glowing in the late afternoon sun, hung from the roofline.

"Does this place seem familiar?" Simon asked.

She shook her head. "I don't know," she said. "I don't know if I recognize it, or if I just like it."

"Two-oh-eight Brooklyn," Simon said. "Let's see who lived there." He shuffled through his notes. "A Mrs. Lula Ford, widow," he said.

Helen shrugged her shoulders. "Doesn't sound familiar." Simon consulted his map as they walked further down the short block. The Millard and the Bradshaw families had lived in the next two homes, and the last one on the street had been vacant when the fire insurance map was drawn.

Brooklyn deadended into Gaston Street. Directly ahead was a single-story gray bungalow with a scarlet front door hung with a holly wreath. The house looked unbalanced compared to the symmetry of the other houses on the street. The right half of the house extended well past the left half, almost touching the sidewalk. A bow-front picture window took up most of the wall facing the street. A porch with Victorian gingerbread trim, added later, Simon was sure, framed the smaller half of the house.

Mutely, Helen pointed forward, then covered her mouth with her hand in a gesture that was becoming very familiar to Simon. He felt his heart rate pick up.

"Who lived there?" she asked.

Simon didn't answer her directly. "Concentrate," he said.

"Well," she said, "I'm thinking, it wasn't always a home? Is that right? It seems so familiar somehow," she said. "Of course, there are thousands of these bungalows all over North Carolina. We have a couple of neighborhoods full of them in Wilmington."

"This was once a duplex with a grocery store in the larger half. W. E. Johnson was the proprietor. His family lived on the other side."

Helen started hopping again. "The store window!" she said. "The one I was looking in! That time I was walking in the snow, was I here?"

"Could be," Simon said.

The two of them turned down Devereaux Street. Helen stopped in front of a stark-white cottage trimmed in dark green. Electric candles lit the two windows off the front porch, where four wooden rockers waited for spring. A very old stone wall, a section of which leaned a bit, surrounded the house. Helen sat down on the wall, and patted the stone.

"This has been here a while."

Simon stood in front of her, messing with his notes again.

"Recognize it?"

"Oh, I don't know," she said, throwing her hands up into the air in a gesture of irritation. "Maybe."

"Edith Donaldson lived here," Simon said.

Helen jumped down off the wall and walked out into the middle of the empty street, rested her fists on her hips, and turned slowly around, inspecting every house on the short block.

"There," she said. "There, that one looks a bit familiar, but hey, like I said, there are thousands of these little bungalows around."

"That was the home of Mrs. May Russell, widow."

Helen sighed in frustration.

"Tired?" Simon asked.

"A little, but I want to keep going."

Simon led her to the left, down Devereaux Street. A square brick building with a clapboard second story and awnings occupied the corner. It was once the Glenwood Knitting Mill. Helen passed right by it.

An ordinary brick church, squat and square, sat on the next corner. The brick was an ugly orange color. Just a touch of detail showed in the tower and door.

"Recognize the church?"

Helen stared at it a long time.

"No," she said. "Should I?"

"Well, yeah, really, you should. It's Jenkins Memorial Church, where the Orphanage children and staff attended services. Annie came here countless times."

Helen stared at it some more.

"Nope," she said. "Nothing."

They walked back to Simon's car.

"It doesn't make sense," Helen said. "Some of it I seemed to recognize, and some I didn't. I don't get it."

"Well," Simon said, starting the engine. "Remember, if you are Annie Evans, and your experiences match those of others with past-incarnation memories, you're not going to remember most of your life. Just a few significant scenes."

"Yeah, but why are they significant? That's what I want to know."

"I did notice something," Simon said.

"What?"

"The houses you paused over — other than the grocery store — widows or single women lived in all of them."

Simon brought the T-bird to a stop in front of his house.

"Got any plans tonight?" Simon asked. "Why don't you come inside for a drink?"

"I'd love to," Helen said. "My motel room is a bit stark. When I'm there, I even forget Christmas is coming."

Once inside, Simon lit the gas fire and went into the kitchen to get white wine for Helen and a beer for himself. Simon's three cats instantly jumped on Helen's lap, kneading her sweater and shedding hair all over her slacks, testing her good nature.

"You have pretty cats," she called out, cupping Cecelia's black and white face in her hands and tickling her long white whiskers. "What are their names?"

"Maybelline, Ruby, and Cecelia," Simon answered. "May is the mother."

"So you're a classic rock 'n' roll fan."

"Who isn't?" Simon asked, handing her a glass of wine. Shooing the cats away, he sat down on the sofa beside her.

"Speaking of Christmas," Simon said. "What will you do if we haven't solved your mystery by then?"

"Well, of course I'll have to go home for Christmas Eve and Christmas Day, at least. My parents expect me. But I'm not due back at work until, I think it's January second this year, so I'll come back and keep looking for answers."

She gazed at him over the top of her wineglass, hesitating.

"You know, if you don't want to help me anymore . . ."

"I couldn't stop now if I wanted to," Simon said. Then, so she wouldn't misinterpret his remark as too personal, he added, "It's such an interesting problem."

She sat her empty wineglass down on the table, after refusing a refill, and tucked her legs under her.

"Do you have an opinion yet?" she asked.

"An opinion on what?" he said.

"Whether or not, well, you know, I was really Annie Evans."

"Annie Evans was a real person. Your memories seem authentic. The kind of recollections you have, how you feel about them, jibes with the most reputable research on past-life memories I can find. Whether the explanation for all this is rational, supernatural, even paranormal, I can't say."

"Are you a religious person? I was raised Presbyterian."

"My mother was Jewish and my father grew up Baptist. My friend Marcus, who's a psychologist as well as a historian, would say I have a personal Judeo-Christian belief system that works for me."

"No room for reincarnation in it?" she said.

"No, but I'm beginning to wonder."

"Really?"

"Really."

"I just want to know that I've done everything I can to get at the truth. Since you've been helping me, I feel confident about that. You haven't been hiding anything from me, have you?"

Simon's expression betrayed him.

She looked at him intently.

"You have! You know something you haven't told me yet, don't you!"

She jumped to her feet, clenching her fists.

"You've got to tell me!"

"Look," Simon said. "I don't want to upset you."

She stamped her foot, furious.

"Don't you dare hide anything from me!"

Simon thought fast. He pulled her down on the sofa next to him. "Okay," he said. "Okay, I'm sorry." Then he told her about John Malone's description of a bug funeral.

"So that's what those children were doing," she said. "I should have thought of something like that. My friends and I used to bury dead birds we found, very solemnly and respectfully, I recall."

Simon relaxed. He could avoid telling her he'd unearthed a baby's corpse, exactly where she'd said it would be, for a while longer.

She leaned in close to him.

"You're not keeping anything else from me, are you?" she asked.

Simon took her face in her hands and kissed her, partly to distract her and partly because he wanted to.

"Well," she said. She didn't pull away from him.

He slipped an arm around her waist.

"You're not engaged to this Henry guy yet, are you?"

"Nearly."

"You're not wearing a ring," Simon said. "That means I can kiss you again."

She didn't object.

He drew her to him and kissed her hard, pulling her onto his lap. He could feel her respond, so he enclosed her in a deep embrace, resting one hand intimately on her hip.

Helen allowed Simon to kiss her for some time, then pulled away from him, straightening her sweater.

"Professor!" she said, smiling. "Who would have guessed!"

"I wouldn't call you bashful, either,"

Simon said. "How long has Henry been at sea?"

He shouldn't have mentioned Henry again.

Discomfort and guilt came between them. Helen, he could tell, felt badly that she'd betrayed her boyfriend, and he worried that he'd compromised his impartiality. Oh, to hell with it, he thought. His attraction to Helen overpowered his scruples, so he endeavored to rekindle the warmth between them.

"Stay for a while," Simon said. "I've got some steaks in the refrigerator, and a stack of movies."

"I shouldn't," Helen said. "Poor Henry. He's out there on that ship, counting cans of peas and boxes of howitzer shells, sharing a bunk with two other guys, and I'm here drinking wine and necking with you in front of a warm fire."

"He's counting peas?"

"No, cans of peas. He's a bookkeeper in the Navy Reserve. He monitors the inventory of an aircraft carrier. His civilian job is in insurance."

"And you said history was boring."

"Pardon me? I don't recall that I meant to insult you. You don't even know Henry."

"Sorry. I'm sure he's a nice guy, if you like him."

Simon knew enough about women not to interfere with Helen's guilt trip. She had to deal with this herself. He didn't mind making her task difficult, though.

"Sure you don't want more wine?" he asked. "One more glass won't hurt. And while I'm in the kitchen, I'll put a couple of baking potatoes in the oven."

Simon's phone rang. He almost let it go, but when he saw the call originated in Florida, he answered it. It was Fred Grimes.

"Hi there," Grimes said. "I recalled something else. I was afraid I'd forget it on the way to my computer, so I picked up the phone."

"What is it?" Simon asked.

"I know exactly when Annie Evans died," Grimes said. "She died on May 5, 1960, the day after Phoebe's twenty-fifth birthday."

"You're sure," Simon said.

"Positive," Grimes said. "I remember the hospital called me, the hospital in Henderson. Annie lived at our lake house, supposedly as caretaker, but really in retirement. Anyway, she'd had a heart attack. The nurse said that Annie was frantic to talk with me, that she had something important to tell me. You see, Stella was on her way out of the country, or Annie would have wanted to see her, not me. I didn't want to go to the hospital that night because I didn't want to miss Phoebe's birthday party. The nurse said Annie was stable and that I could wait until the next day. Well, the nurse was wrong. When I arrived at the hospital the next morning, Annie had just died."

"Fred, thanks so much for calling," Simon said. "This could be very helpful."

"I can't believe I didn't remember sooner," Fred said. "It always bothered me that I didn't go to her right away, as many years as she worked for our family. For a long time, I wondered what it was she wanted to tell me."

"Do you know where she was buried?"

"Oh, hell. I should know exactly where. It took all the money she had to bury her, I remember that much. My secretary may have handled it. Damn it! Don't ever get this old. It's so frustrating. I know Annie didn't have a will, because I do recall that I didn't know where to send her personal belongings. Not that she had much. Maybe I gave it all to charity."

"Please keep trying to remember more."

"Sure. Gives me something else to think of besides regularity. Oh, and I did call

Phoebe and insist that she vote tomorrow to give you access to the Orphanage archives. She's convinced you're a liberal in sheep's clothing, you know, trying to scuttle Lucius' campaign."

"Kind of makes you wonder what it is she thinks I might find."

"That's exactly what I told her."

With Fred's permission, Helen had listened to the conversation on an extension. She phoned for a pizza while Simon booted up his computer. On the Social Security records Web site he entered Annie's name and date of death. He got a match. He turned the computer so Helen could read it. In the blanks reserved for date of birth and place of birth, "UNK," for "unknown" was entered.

"Damn it," Helen said. "How can someone not know when and where she was born?"

"Oh, Annie knew," Simon said. "This just means that she didn't have a birth certificate. Say she was born in the late 1880s. The state didn't keep birth records. And her death certificate, obviously, would have been filled out after her death, when they couldn't ask her."

"So we'll never know where she's from?"

"We need to get into the Orphanage archives. They may have letters or other documents that tell us. And it seems to me that if that little magazine, the *Raleigh Christian Messenger*, published a story about her when she was hired, it might have published an obituary, too. She must have been a member of a church — I don't think the Orphanage would have hired her otherwise. If an obituary mentions her home church, we might find more records there."

"If the church still exists. When can we get into the archives?"

"I don't know. The board of the Children's Foundation has to vote to give me access, then I need to find out where the records are. The board meets at ten tomorrow morning, so maybe I'll know by noon."

"Can I go with you?"

"Sure. I'll say you're my research assistant, if I have to."

The pizza arrived. Between bites, Simon and Helen went over what they knew about Annie. When they were finished, Simon's notes filled less than a page.

"Not much of a life," Helen said. "It's depressing."

"You know what I wonder?" Simon asked. "I wonder what it was Annie was so desperate to tell Fred Grimes."

"Me, too," Helen said. "Could that be Annie's 'unfinished business,' the reason I have these memories of her life, my life?" She pulled at her dark hair in mock annoyance, tousling it in the process. When she lifted her arms, her sweater rode up and Simon could see her midriff. A small gold ring pierced her navel. It took every ounce of restraint Simon had to keep himself from taking her in his arms again. She was a client, despite what had happened between them earlier in the evening, and until he was finished helping her, he resolved once again to stay impartial. Of course, if she made a move, he couldn't be expected to resist.

She didn't. Instead, Helen insisted on walking back to the motel by herself. It was still early, her way lit by streetlamps and Christmas lights, but he asked her to call him just to make sure she arrived safely. Ten minutes or so later, as Simon locked up his house, she called. Simon told her he'd let her know just as soon as he heard whether or not they could get into the Orphanage's archives.

"What if you can't?" she asked.

"I think we can," he said. "Let's just wait and see what happens next."

Simon was brushing his teeth, and his cats

were circling their usual sleeping spots on his bed, when the phone rang again. Maybe Helen had remembered something else, he thought, but when he picked up the receiver an unfamiliar, elderly woman's voice spoke.

"Are you Professor Simon Shaw?" she asked. She said his name slowly, as if she was reading it.

"Yes, I am," Simon said.

"I'm Gloria Fitzhugh," she said. "I live in the next door apartment to Lorena Henly."

Simon felt a sense of foreboding descend on him.

"Is she all right?" Simon asked.

"I'm afraid not. She passed this afternoon."

"I'm so sorry."

"We were supposed to go to dinner. A big group of us were going to the K&W Cafeteria. Lorena wasn't in the lobby when we arranged to meet, and when I went upstairs to get her I knocked and knocked at her door. I called the manager, who unlocked her door, and there she was, sitting in her rocking chair, looking like she'd fallen asleep watching television."

"I'm sorry," Simon said again. He didn't know what else to say. Miss Henly was over ninety years old. As his Aunt Rae always said, usually while she was trying to get him to go to church, no one gets out of this world alive.

"I saw your card on her counter, and I thought maybe you all had an appointment or something," Gloria said.

"No, Ma'am. I was chatting with Miss Henly about her childhood at the Raleigh Christian Orphanage. I left the card in case she wanted to call me later."

"She'd been eating a bowl of vanilla ice cream," Gloria said. "The empty bowl was still sitting in her lap."

Simon's cats slept much better than Simon did that night.

Simon was in his office at the college by eight, when he called the Raleigh Christian Foundation. He spoke to the executive director, Donald Peters, who verified that Simon's request to do research in the Orphanage's archives was on the agenda of the Board of Directors' meeting.

"There shouldn't be any problem," Peters said. "We've granted two requests like yours in the past. I think we should donate the archives to a university library. They just collect dust and cost us storage fees."

"The two requests you got before mine — can you tell me who they were?"

"Sure. One was a graduate student writing a paper on the orphanage movement. The second was trying to locate a great-grandparent for a genealogy, I believe."

"Was either one of them a woman in her mid-twenties, with dark brown hair?"

"Nope. Both were men."

"Thanks. Can I call you around lunchtime?"

"Oh, I'll call you. I don't mind."

Once off the telephone, Simon could turn his attention to the three notes that had been slipped under his door. What a nuisance.

He opened the first, unfolding a plea hand-printed in red ink on lined paper.

"Dear Professor Shaw," it read. *"My family lives in a mobile home in order to afford to send me to Kenan College . . ."* Simon groaned, refolding the note without finishing it. He wrote the day's date on the outside.

He opened the second appeal, neatly printed out on heavy bond paper.

"Dear Dr. Shaw," it began. *"I'm very interested in historical fiction. I've had two stories published already, one in* Western Stories *and one in* Old Texas Tales. *I specialize in gunfights and hangings. Taking your course would . . ."*

Simon couldn't stand it. He stuffed all the notes into his waiting list file, skimming the third just long enough to make sure it was a request for admission to the seminar rather than something more important, like a Christmas party invitation. Please Lord, he thought, don't let any of my preregistered students drop out of this seminar, or I'll have to admit one of these imbeciles.

After proctoring his North Carolina History exam, Simon stuffed the stack of blue books into his briefcase and wandered into the lounge. He took his cell phone with him in case Peters called him, although it was a little early to expect it. Marcus and Sophie sat on the sofa, Marcus correcting blue books at the speed of sound, Sophie propping her feet up on the coffee table and resting a paperback edition of *Dr. Spock's Baby and Child Care* on her stomach.

"Still here?" Simon asked her.

"Not for long," she said. "I'm two centimeters dilated."

"Don't get your hopes up," Marcus said to her. "My wife carried our third for two weeks at three centimeters. The baby dropped so low she could hardly walk."

"Way too much information," Simon said. "Spare me. Just let me know when the baby's arrived so I can get her a nice gift and come over and admire her."

"How's your project?" Marcus asked.

"What project?" Simon asked.

"Sophie and I both know, remember?" Marcus said.

"I can still get you those references on Holocaust past-life memories," Sophie said.

"One past incarnation is enough," Simon said. "But seriously, guys, Helen's story is compelling."

"Do you think it's true?" Sophie asked. "Keep good notes. I want to read them when you're finished."

Simon knew that he could count on the two of them not to gossip, and he needed to talk.

"I think there could be something to her story," he said.

"There's one born every day, they say," Marcus said.

"You believe in the miracle of the loaves and the fishes," Simon said. "That's hard for some people to swallow, you know."

"That's different."

"How is it different?" Sophie said.

"Our beliefs, Jewish and Christian, are grounded in the Bible, much of which is historically verifiable, and in the prehistory of the Middle East. We can't prove the loaves and fishes, but we do know that Jesus preached to a huge crowd on the Sea of Galilee. And we're pretty sure Moses existed. But there's no evidence to support reincarnation . . ."

"Siddhartha was a historical person, too, and what about the countless individuals who remember a previous life, some of them with amazing accuracy," Sophie said. "I'm only familiar with the Holocaust literature, but I'm eager to see Simon's results." She winced. "Oof," she said. "I believe my daughter was an acrobat in her past incarnation."

Simon's cell rang. It was Donald Peters. The board of the Foundation had approved his request, and he could come by the office and pick up the keys to the storage unit where the archives were stored. Peters gave him directions to the Foundation's office. On his way out of the building, Simon stopped at the vending machines to get a Coke and a pack of Nabs for lunch.

The Raleigh Christian Foundation was housed in a modern glass building just off Glenwood Avenue. Simon scanned the list of offices on the directory mounted next to the elevator. He noticed that the Grimes

Family Trust had its offices two floors below the Foundation's fifth-floor headquarters.

The Foundation's suite contained only Donald Peters' office, a secretary's desk in the reception area, and an elegant conference room, which had just been vacated by the board. A door in the conference room opened into a tiny kitchenette, where a sterling silver coffee service, china plates, and crumpled cloth napkins crowded a small counter. Scribbled-on agendas, empty Perrier bottles, and ornate pens were scattered all over the conference table. Oil portraits hung on every wall. Peters pointed one out to Simon.

"He was the last director of the Orphanage," Peters said. "During his term, he was wise enough to understand that orphanages were going out of fashion. It was his idea to sell the orphanage property and use the proceeds to fund the Foundation."

"I know the campus sold for a small fortune."

"There's almost thirty million dollars in the endowment," Peters said.

"The Foundation benefits children's organizations?"

"Foster child services, adoption of special needs children, college scholarships, camps."

"The Grimes family has always been involved?"

"Yes, Stella Grimes Lay was cared for in the orphanage when her mother was widowed. Her life was saved by one of the matrons."

Our Annie Evans, Simon thought.

"Her family has always been grateful," Peters said.

Peters rummaged around in his desk. He pulled out a credit card–sized key card and a large traditional brass key and handed them to Simon.

"The archives are stored in that big storage facility out on Glenwood Avenue," Peters said. "It's climate controlled, automated, and very secure. Often there are no employees in the building. But the card opens the main door, and the key admits you to our locker on the second floor. The documents are organized in file boxes. Tell me, what are you looking for again?"

Simon almost forgot his excuse. "A friend of mine is trying to find out about a relative who worked at the Orphanage in the early part of the twentieth century."

"Keep the keys as long as you like," Peters said, losing interest in Simon. He started to clean up the mess on the conference table, already thinking about the rest of his day.

"Tell me one thing," Simon said. "Did the entire board vote to let me use the records?"

"All but Phoebe Hays," Peters said.

"That surprises me," Simon said, recalling that Fred Grimes had called his daughter to urge her to vote affirmatively.

Peters shrugged. "Mrs. Hays is always a bit contrary. It's her nature. That's just between us," Peters added. "It was a frustrating meeting. Interest rates are down, and we couldn't afford to give as much money this year as last."

On an impulse, Simon dropped by the Grimes Family Trust offices on the way out of the building. The receptionist's desk was empty. Lucius Hays poked his head out of a nearby office when he heard the front door open and close.

"Wait just a minute, if you would," he said. "I'll be done here in jiff." He ducked back into his office and closed the door.

To pass the time while he waited for Lucius, Simon looked over the pictures hanging on the wall. A few of the photographs were taken at the turn of the century, when the Grimes family settled in Raleigh. One showed an Edwardian gentleman in coat and tie, with black cuff protectors, posing stiffly behind the counter of a primitive auto parts store. Another depicted the same gentleman with a young boy behind the wheel of a Model T Runabout. Could they be Fred Grimes and his father? Yet another photograph revealed a rustic Victorian country house with a long dock leading out to water. A canoe was tied up at the dock, and Simon could just make out a couple of bathers in knee-length swimwear sitting on the dock, dangling their toes.

"Professor Shaw? Can I help you with something?" Lucius said, leaving his office and stretching out a hand for Simon to shake. Lucius looked deliberately casual, as if he was prepared for a photographer to pop up at a moment's notice to take a candid shot. His dress shirt sleeves were rolled up so evenly someone must have helped him do it. Behind him, sitting around a conference table in his office, Simon could see men in dark business suits waiting for Lucius to return. The men must be politicos and potential contributors, Simon thought, the impression coming unbidden into his mind.

"I saw the Grimes trust on the building directory and just dropped by," Simon said, wishing he'd thought of a better excuse. "I was upstairs at the Foundation's office to get the keys to the Orphanage archives."

"Ah yes," Lucius said, folding his arms.

"My mother told me. You're determined to insinuate yourself into our family's affairs, aren't you?"

"I'm only interested in Annie Evans," Simon said.

"Whatever," Lucius said, looking backward into his office. "I need to get back to my meeting. Jesse's down the hall, if you want to say hello."

"Sure," Simon said. "Why not?"

Jesse sat at a handsome mahogany desk, leaning back in a black leather chair, surfing the Internet on his computer. When he saw Simon, he quickly exited and shut down, tipping his chair up and turning to face him. The computer screen went blue before Simon could see what he'd been doing.

"Hey," Jesse said. "What's up?"

"Nothing much," Simon said. "I saw your office, and stopped in on impulse." Very lame, Simon thought.

"Sit," Jesse said.

Simon sat.

"I've got a lunch date in half an hour. I'm just killing time. Lucius gets upset with me if I don't show up here every few days."

"Your cousin is a serious man," Simon said.

"Serious about getting elected," Jesse said. "He wants it to appear like the family works for a living. It's silly — the trust department at the bank takes care of everything. He just uses the office for meetings. But I come in anyway, a couple times a week, for appearances sake. So, what are you doing in the building?"

Simon told him about getting access to the Orphanage's archives, and needing to pick up the keys.

"Phoebe doesn't want me to go over there, I don't think," Simon said. "Lucius either."

Jesse shrugged. "Doesn't bother me. I can't imagine what would interest anyone among all those boxes of old papers. Makes my allergies act up just to think about it."

Jesse was bored with the conversation, and so was Simon. There was nothing to talk to this man about. What did he do with his time? Go to parties and football games? At least Lucius and Phoebe had goals, and worked at meeting them, even if they didn't need to make a living.

"Well," Simon said. "I'm off."

"See you," Jesse said. He powered up his computer as Simon left his office.

It seemed preordained that Simon would run into all of Stella Grimes Lay's relatives today. Just as he rounded the corner to the bank of elevators, one elevator door opened and Phoebe stepped out.

"Well," she said. "How are you, Dr. Shaw? You must have come by to get the keys to the archives."

"Yeah," Simon said. "And I stopped by the Grimes trust offices, too.

"Then you've spoken to Lucius? You've heard about John Malone?"

"I saw Lucius, but he didn't mention John."

Simon knew what she was going to say. He could tell from her expression. She had composed her face to deliver bad news without much caring about it herself.

"He's dead," she said.

9

I've been born more times than Krishna.

— MARK TWAIN

"What happened?" Simon asked.

"He fell down the steps of his apartment. Lucius found him when he went out to the garage this morning."

"I'm sorry. It must have been a shock."

"The police came. And an ambulance. And the media. Because it's Lucius' home, of course. What a mess."

How inconvenient for you, Simon thought.

"John was drunk, of course. His body reeked of bourbon. He always went on a bender when his wife was out of town. I've spent the morning trying to get in touch with her. Finally found her. She was coming home today, on the train, but now she and her daughter are driving."

Phoebe moved away from him into the corridor.

"I'm sorry," she said. "I have to go. I'm late."

Simon found himself at his car without remembering how he got there. He felt shaken. Two people he'd talked to just two days ago, Lorena Henly and John Malone, were dead. Sure they were old, but their deaths were still shocking. Their deaths couldn't be related to his investigation, could they? After all, Phoebe had denied knowing anyone who had worked for Stella, all the while Malone was living over her garage. Why didn't she want Simon to talk to him? Did she know Simon had interviewed Lorena Henly? What could Phoebe be hiding? Or Lucius, or Jesse, for that matter?

Simon drove, five miles over the speed limit, to the Glenwood Arms, the apartments for the elderly where Miss Henly had lived. He parked and got out, waiting for two oldsters wearing elf hats and driving mobile carts with American flags flying, to scoot past him out the entrance. Inside the empty foyer, he searched fruitlessly for surveillance cameras. Then he went up the elevator alone, and found himself in Miss Henly's corridor. There wasn't a soul in sight. No cameras here, either. A black wreath hung on Miss Henly's door. The door of Gloria Fitzhugh's neighboring apartment displayed a sign that read: "Hard of hearing. Doorbell activates flashing light. Please wait."

Someone could have walked into the apartment building and knocked on Miss Henly's door without being seen, that much was clear.

Simon rang Gloria's doorbell and waited, as instructed. A few minutes later Gloria answered her door. She was a sweet-looking woman, not as elderly as Miss Henly. She wore a tailored black dress and had soft red hair, carefully tended, with no gray roots showing.

"You're Professor Shaw," Gloria said, reaching for his hand, then leading him into her apartment. It was the mirror image of Miss Henly's, a living room with kitchenette and a bedroom beyond. "I recognize you from your picture in the newspaper last summer," Gloria said.

"I just saw Miss Henly on Saturday."

"I know," she said. "Here, sit in this chair, this is my good ear."

Simon sat down and leaned toward Mrs. Fitzhugh, raising his voice.

"I came by, well, to express sympathy, and to ask if Miss Henly had any visitors yesterday?"

"Not that I know of. I don't hear well, you see. She didn't have any children. No one to bury her. We, her friends, are taking care of everything." Gloria sniffled, dabbing at her nose with a handkerchief.

"This might seem intrusive to you, Mrs. Fitzhugh, but do you know if there's going to be a post-mortem? I know Miss Henly was elderly, but her death seemed so sudden."

"Interesting that you should ask that," Gloria said. "There will be an autopsy. Apparently the coroner thinks Lorena committed suicide."

Simon took a few seconds to compose himself.

"Why would she do that? She didn't seem depressed to me."

"Not to me, either. She loved life. Always watching the new shows on television, going to the mall and out to eat. But you see, her medications — for sleeping and pain — the bottles were empty. And they weren't due to be refilled for a couple of weeks. She had cancer, you know."

"No, I didn't."

"Our manager here, he's a nice boy, but someone that young can't know much about life yet, can he? He said Lorena got tired of living and didn't want to die in pain. I don't believe it."

"Why not?"

"We were going to the K&W Cafeteria. Lorena loved their fried chicken livers. If she was going to commit suicide, she would have done it after dinner."

Simon fretted while he drove to Helen's motel. Lorena Henly and John Malone hadn't died of causes that one would think of as "normal" in an elderly person, like a heart attack, or a stroke, but one from a serious accident and another by suicide. Phoebe's opposition to his research in the Orphanage's archives bothered him, too. He could understand why she didn't want him to rummage around in her attic, but why on earth would she care what he might discover in the archives? She went against her father's express wishes by voting against allowing him access to the Orphanage's records. Maybe she just wanted him barred from access to any information related to her family. It seemed ridiculous, since after Lucius' nomination, professional journalists would start circling the Hays family like sharks, looking for the tiniest flaw. If there was a family secret, surely they'd find it eventually. Simon realized he didn't like any of them, except maybe Fred, whom he had never met.

He told Helen about John Malone and

Lorena Henly as soon as he picked her up.

"It's got to be a coincidence," she said. "Their deaths couldn't have anything to do with me or Annie. No one knew we were going to talk to Miss Henly except the Webbs. And you told me Mr. Malone didn't have any useful information about Annie."

"You're probably right."

She was right, Simon thought. His dabbling in murder cases had made him overly suspicious. If there were skeletons in the Grimes closet, Malone hadn't told anyone about them yet, so why would he now? It wouldn't make sense for Phoebe or Lucius to "remove" Malone so close to the election, when attention was focused on the family. No one else, except Wade, and he didn't count, knew that Simon and Helen were doing anything other than a little harmless genealogical research. The Grimes family simply didn't want the two of them meddling in their family history because of Lucius' run for the Senate, that's all. Miss Henly killed herself because she had cancer, and Malone fell down a steep set of stairs when drunk. Simon wasn't surprised he'd been drinking. The man had been half-plastered when Simon visited him.

They stopped at a convenience store on

their way to the storage facility.

"Have you ever spent hours sorting through cartons of stored documents?" Simon asked. "We need water, snacks, gloves, and antihistamines."

The storage facility was a vast, windowless, concrete block building. Simon rang the buzzer of the electric blue front door next to a loading dock. There was no answer, so he inserted the card key into the lock. The metal security door opened smoothly, then shut behind them. No one was in the reception or office areas. The building was quiet as an empty church, except for the whoosh of the ventilation system and an occasional electronic beep. A long hall ran down the center of the building. Solid metal doors spaced every ten feet or so opened into the storage units on either side.

"There's no one here," Helen said. Her voice echoed. "How can it be safe?"

"I'm sure there are motion detectors, smoke alarms, and security cameras, probably monitored by somebody in Duluth. Who needs human beings in this day and age?"

"I'm not getting on the elevator. What if it gets stuck between floors?"

"There's an alarm in there, too," Simon said.

They took the stairs anyway.

They found the correct storage unit. The brass key opened the lock smoothly and silently, and the door closed behind them, clicking shut. Helen started.

"We're not locked in, are we?" Helen said.

"Of course not," Simon said. He opened the door with the key to show her, then closed it again, then opened it. "See? No problem."

"Sorry," she said. "I'm a little claustrophobic."

Simon flipped the light switch next to the door, and a bank of fluorescent lights overhead flickered on. The corrugated blue metal walls of the unit rose to about ten feet in height. An HVAC duct set in the floor, fire sprinklers in the ceiling, and a tiny ventilation window covered in wire mesh on an outside wall were the only breaks in the institutional squareness of the space.

The unit was about five hundred square feet, lined with metal shelves loaded with file boxes. A couple of metal tables stood in the center of the room, stacked with a jumble of miscellaneous items, including clothing, that wouldn't fit in file boxes.

"What a mess," Helen said. She lifted a maroon letter jacket embroidered with "RCO" in gold felt letters.

"Malone said the Orphanage had a good football team," Simon said.

"Here's a baseball trophy," Helen said, holding up a statuette of a batter waiting at home plate for a pitch. "1972."

She sneezed once, then again. "I hope these allergy pills work soon," she said.

"Let's get into the documents," Simon said. "The boxes aren't labeled. This could take all afternoon. Annie was hired in 1909, and left in 1930. So we're looking for papers from those years. And from 1960, when she died, in case the Orphanage noted it in some way," Simon said.

"Try the boxes that look the most beat up the first," Helen said. "They should be the oldest."

"Nice idea, but they're identical. All the papers must have been packed at one time, before they were stored. Make sure to put on your gloves, or you'll hurt your hands."

Methodically they worked their way around the room, lifting down each box and carefully checking the dates of the documents inside. The boxes contained an assortment of records like official letters, scrapbooks, photo albums, school literary magazines, photographs, menus, newspaper clippings, even band music.

"Bingo, 1912!" Helen said. Eagerly they went through the box, one document at a time. "Here's the menu for Easter dinner," Simon said. "Ham, sweet potatoes, rolls, collards, and coconut cake."

"And here's a memo from the director complaining about relatives of the kids giving them spending money when they should be giving it to the Orphanage for their maintenance," Helen said. "He also says the relatives visit too much. It disrupts their routine."

None of the documents mentioned Annie Evans. Simon and Helen repacked the box and lifted it back onto the shelf.

After two hours, they had found nothing. Helen pulled off her dusty gloves and massaged her hands, then the back of her neck.

"Time for a break," Simon said. They sat with their backs to a shelf and drank bottled water and nibbled on peanut butter crackers.

"This is very discouraging," Helen said.

"We can't give up. We have to go through every single box, the last as patiently as the first. If we don't find anything today, there's tomorrow and the day after that."

Many boxes later, Simon checked his watch. It was almost six o'clock. They had found two references to Annie. A 1929 issue of the *Raleigh Christian Messenger* contained a photo of two Orphanage girls who won a sewing prize at the state fair under Annie's tutelage. The other mention occurred in a letter expelling a child who was a discipline problem.

"We should go get some dinner," Simon said. "We'll come back first thing to-morrow."

"Just one more box," Helen said. "That'll finish off this shelf."

The two of them slid the box off a lower shelf, and Helen lifted the lid and pulled out a file folder stuffed with papers. Her hand began to tremble. "1960!" she shouted, her voice ringing out, echoing off the metal walls.

"Copies of the *Raleigh Christian Messenger* for 1960," she said, holding up a stack of magazines. "You look, I can't," she said, handing them over to Simon. Simon sat cross-legged on the floor and began to leaf through them.

"Let's see, Fred said Annie died on May 5, 1960," Simon said.

"I'm going over here to this corner to hy-perventilate," Helen said, crossing the room and crouching on the floor with her hands over her eyes. "If you don't find anything, I'm calling the whole thing off," she said, her voice muffled by her hands. "I can't take the stress."

"Hot damn," Simon said. "Got it," he said, waving an issue of a newsletter over his head in Helen's general direction. "Annie Evans' obituary!"

"Oh, God," Helen said, running over to Simon and dropping down next to him. She put her hands over her face again. "Read it to me," she said. Simon did.

Annie Evans, matron of the Baby Cottage of the Raleigh Christian Orphanage from 1909 to 1930, Dies in Henderson

Annie Evans, the first matron of the RCO Baby Cottage, died of heart failure on May 5, 1960, in Henderson, North Carolina, where she was semi-retired, living in the vacation home of her employers, Stella Grimes Lay and her brother, Fred Grimes. Mrs. Evans came to the Orphanage after the tragic death of her husband, Leonard Ames Evans, in a house fire, with the highest recommendation of her pastor at the Fuquay Memorial Methodist Church, where her family attended services for many years.

Mrs. Evans was born Annie Moffat in what was then Sippihaw, now Fuquay Springs, North Carolina, on May 4, 1888. She attended the first white school built between Raleigh and Fayetteville until her graduation from the eighth grade. In June of 1906, she married Leonard Evans. The couple worked his family farm until his death, when the farm reverted to the ownership of the deceased's brother. Mrs. Evans worked briefly at the Fuquay Mineral Springs Hotel until her felicitous arrival at the Orphanage.

For the past thirty years, Mrs. Evans worked as a nanny, then housekeeper, for Stella Grimes Lay, one of her charges during her years at the Baby Cottage. The story of their acquaintance is one of legends of the Orphanage. Mrs. Lay came to the Orphanage as an eighteen-month-old infant. During her required two week quarantine in the infirmary, she was afflicted with measles, then pneumonia. Mrs. Evans, who had survived measles during her own childhood, offered to nurse the girl during her desperate illness, which was then so often fatal. Mrs. Lay survived, and after she returned to her family, then married, she brought Mrs. Evans into her home to care for her own child. The Grimes and Lay families became long-time benefactors of the Orphanage.

Mrs. Annie Evans was buried in the cemetery of her home church in Fuquay Springs.

"I don't believe it," Helen said. "It's her."

She took the magazine out of Simon's hand, read the obituary again, then clutched the magazine to her chest.

"What do we do now?" she asked.

"Go to Fuquay, or rather, Fuquay-Varina and the Methodist church there. But not until morning. I need a beer and a steak."

Simon took the magazine from Helen, folded it, and stuffed it in his jacket pocket.

"Can you take that?"

"There're several copies of this issue, and besides, I'll return it."

They collected their stuff and made sure they'd left the storage unit as tidy as they'd found it. Simon inserted the key into the door. It wouldn't turn. He took the key out, reinserted it, and twisted it confidently. It still wouldn't turn. Then he shoved on the door, trying to jiggle it and work the key at the same time.

"What's wrong?" Helen said. "Won't the door open?"

"Of course it will open," Simon said. "It engaged smooth as silk the last time I tried it."

He took the key out of the lock and examined it, as if to reassure himself that he was using the right one. The large brass key wasn't bent or twisted. He inserted it in the lock again. Not only wouldn't the key turn, it didn't even seem to penetrate as far as it should into the lock.

"This is nuts," Simon said.

"Let me try," Helen said.

Helen tried the key twice. It didn't work.

"We're not trapped here," Helen said. "Are we?"

"Of course not. Let me try again."

After several more attempts, one after the other, they admitted to themselves that the door wasn't going to open. The unit hadn't seemed confining all afternoon, but now Simon wanted out of it in the worst way.

"How about trying the credit card thing," Helen said. "You know, slide the card in, push the bolt back?"

Simon shook his head. "The dead bolt is an inch long." He tried it anyway. His credit card wouldn't even slip through the crack between the doorjamb and the door.

"Okay," Simon said. "Let's think. Cell phone first." He turned his phone on. No service.

"Let me try mine," Helen said. "I use a different carrier." She didn't have service either. The two of them scrambled all over the unit, including getting under the tables and climbing to the top of the shelving, trying to find a spot where one of their phones would work. Simon gave up and stuffed his phone back in his jacket pocket.

"Is there a fire alarm?" Helen asked. "You know, one of those glass boxes with an axe and a switch to pull?" The two of them combed the storage unit again, peering behind shelving and moving boxes, looking for an alarm or a panic button. They found nothing.

Simon swore. Helen pushed her damp bangs back from her forehead. Then she swore, too.

"Now I'm truly hungry and thirsty," she said. "Is there any more water?"

"One bottle," Simon said. "But we'd better save it. We don't know how long it might be until we get out of here."

"I guess we could be stuck here all night," Helen said. "Or longer, if no one decides to come check on their stuff."

"There have to be employees here sometime," Simon said. He went to the door and beat on it, shouting. Helen joined him. They made a terrific amount of noise, but no one came. Then Simon tried the lock again.

"I don't understand it," he said. "This is a new security lock, the kind that's guaranteed for a lifetime. It should work."

"Well, it doesn't." Helen glanced at the ceiling, at the sprinklers. Simon followed her gaze. He knew what she was thinking.

"They do it on television all the time," she said.

"I don't smoke," he said. "Do you have any matches?"

"Just what I pick up from restaurants," she said, digging around in her pocketbook until she found a tiny matchbook with four matches in it.

The two of them piled boxes on top of one of the metal tables. Simon climbed carefully up the rickety tower until he could reach the ceiling. He lit the matches one by one, holding them directly on a sprinkler head until each had burned out.

"I don't hear an alarm," Helen said.

"Must not be hot enough."

Simon climbed back down and jumped from the table to the floor.

"Okay," Helen said. "I want to get out of here. Now."

They sat on the floor and each swallowed

a few mouthfuls of water.

"I've got a package of Nabs," Simon said.

"I've got a tube of cashews and half a chocolate bar," Helen said.

"Let's save them."

"Knowing I can't eat or drink anything just makes me hungrier and thirstier," Helen said. She noticed him staring at the tiny ventilation window in the outside wall.

"I don't think one of your cats could fit through that opening."

"I'm going to climb up and holler out," Simon said.

"Like anyone can hear you. There's a very noisy four-lane street on that side of the building, and a row of pine trees between the building and the road."

Simon did it anyway, climbing carefully up a section of metal shelving while Helen held it steady, and yelling until he was hoarse.

They didn't know what else to do, except sit back down and share a few more swallows of water and eat two peanut butter crackers each.

"Crap," Simon said. He went over to the heavy metal door and threw his weight on it. It didn't even shiver.

"I don't know how this situation could get much worse," he said.

The lights went out. Simon groped his way to the light switch, and flicked it on and off several times.

"The lights must be on an automatic timer to save power," Simon said.

He felt Helen's hand on his shoulder. "What time is it?"

"Nine," he said, reading the luminescent dial of his watch. He slid down the door until he sat on the floor.

"God damn it," he said. He longed to be at home, watching bad shows on cable television, shooing his cats away from his popcorn.

Helen joined him on the floor.

"There must be something else we can do," she said.

"Not in the dark," he said. "We'll have to wait until morning."

"We will get out," Helen said. "I've never heard of anyone dying in a storage unit. The heat's still on, and our water will last a while. We'll think of something, or someone will come rescue us."

"Of course," Simon said, though he was convinced of just the opposite. They could live for a long time without food, but just three or four days without water. Only luck in the form of a human being happening onto the second-floor hallway of the storage building could prevent them from dying there.

They made a bed of sorts out of the collection of letter jackets that were piled on the tables in the middle of the room. They curled up together, covered by their coats. Simon wrapped his arms around her.

"For warmth," he said. He snuggled his head into her neck.

Helen sighed theatrically. "Men," she said.

Simon kissed her neck. Several times. She didn't stop him until he moved his hands.

"You're all alike," she said. "As soon as we knew we might be trapped in here, you started to obsess about sex, and how much you could get before you're too weak from hunger and thirst to go on."

"Well . . . ," Simon said.

"Tell you what," Helen said. "I promise that if death seems imminent, I'll put out. Until then, don't bother me. Just keep me warm."

"Whatever you say."

A few moments passed.

"Cut it out," she said.

"I can't help it. It's biology. How do you think six billion people got onto this earth? Not because men are hard to arouse."

Helen snorted.

"Women exchange sex and children for food and shelter," Simon said. "This efficient arrangement is embedded in our genes. Why fight it?"

"The food and shelter you've provided me with tonight stink," Helen said. "I'm not exchanging a damn thing for them. Stop pestering me and go to sleep."

Simon rolled over so that their backs faced.

"You must admit you're not bored."

"Hush. Stop piffling."

A few more minutes passed.

"This isn't helping me," he said. She didn't answer. "Helen?" She snored softly in reply.

It was a couple of hours before Simon could fall asleep. While he waited, he contemplated the starry sky through the slits in the ventilation duct on the outside wall of the storage unit. Before he finally drifted off, he had figured out how to get out of the unit, but he had to wait until morning. He needed light to keep from breaking his neck.

The fluorescent lights flashed on, their soft buzzing filling the quiet room. Simon was already on his feet, standing underneath the ventilation duct. Helen awoke rubbing her eyes, stretching stiff muscles.

"Good morning," Simon said.

"Good morning. God, I would kill for a cup of coffee and an Egg McMuffin. Do we have any peanut butter crackers left?"

"Come over here," Simon said. "I need your help. We'll get that coffee and Egg McMuffin on the way home."

"What are you thinking?" Helen asked, coming to Simon's side and following his gaze upward to the ventilation duct. "You can't possibly get out there."

"I just need my arm."

"What are you going to do, wave to the traffic? No one will notice, not to mention the trees between us and the road . . ."

"Hold on to the shelf while I climb up," Simon said.

Helen humored him, bracing her feet on the floor while she leaned against the shelving unit.

Simon reached the top shelf, unfolded the screwdriver blade from his pocket knife, and unscrewed the vent cover. It didn't take long. He tossed the cover over Helen's head onto the floor.

"Okay," Helen said. "Why not? You wave as long as you can, then I'll take over."

Simon pulled out his cell phone, clicked the power button, and extended the phone as far as his arm could reach outside the vent. He had service.

The building manager's master key wouldn't open the unit's lock either, so the nice policeman called a locksmith, who, after less destructive attempts to force the lock, resorted to an acetylene torch to cut through the dead bolt. Simon watched from the inside of the unit while the flame slowly sliced through metal. When the door opened, he and Helen bolted into the hall. The policeman offered him a bottle of water. Freed from the requirement to conserve, Simon drained it. He hadn't realized how thirsty he was.

"I'm so sorry," the manager said. The man couldn't have been more than twenty. His skin was still in the aftermath of adolescence, and his goatee was a bit thin in places. "I don't understand how this could have happened. These locks are supposed to be foolproof."

"It's okay," Helen said. "We got out, that's the important thing."

"No, it's not okay," the manager said. "You've been, ah, inconvenienced, to say the least. I'll call the corporate office today and ask about compensation. At least let me buy you breakfast."

"We just want to go home," Helen said. "Simon's car is right outside."

While Helen dealt with the manager, Simon watched the locksmith examine the lock, which he had cut free of the door. He jiggled it, trying Simon's key and then the manager's.

"Very odd," he said. He gave the policeman the lock. "If I were you, I'd turn this over to your forensics guys. It could have been tampered with."

"I'm sure that's not the case," the manager said, alarmed. "Sometimes locks fail. This building is completely secure."

"These two," the policeman said, nodding at Simon and Helen, "could have died."

"Oh, no," the manager said. "Surely not."

"Whatever," the policeman said. "Don't come near this unit until the lab is done with the lock."

Simon and Helen drove into the car service area of the first McDonald's they saw on the way home and ordered a coffee and a bag of assorted breakfast foods.

"Want to stop at my house?" Simon said.

"No, thanks," Helen said. "I want to get back to my room and take a long, hot shower."

Simon dropped her off and went on home.

When he pulled up, he saw an unmarked Raleigh police car parked out front. Otis Gates sat in the front seat, smoking a cigarette.

"Hey," Otis said, getting out of his car to greet Simon. His cigarette was smoked down almost to the filter. Otis only allowed himself three fags per day, and got the most out of each one. He drew a last lungful of smoke and expelled it, then dropped the butt on the sidewalk and crushed it with his foot.

"Hey yourself," Simon answered.

"You okay? I heard what happened."

"I'm fine, or I will be after I take a shower."

"Those cats of yours are raising hell inside."

"They're hungry, I expect. Come on in. Let me feed them, then I'll make coffee. Do you have time to take a break and have some with me?"

"Certainly. I've got all the time I need. I'm on official business."

10

> I adopted the theory of Reincarnation when I was twenty-six. Religion offered nothing to the point. Even work could not give me complete satisfaction. Work is futile if we cannot utilize the experience we collect in one life in the next.
>
> — HENRY FORD

Simon handed Otis a mug of black coffee, then slurped at his own, so thick with sugar and cream it resembled a chocolate milkshake.

"So what's this official business? I thought I'd already made my donation to the Police Fund this year," Simon said.

Otis drew out a slim notebook and a chrome pen from his inside jacket pocket. He flipped through the notebook until he found a blank page, and scribbled the date on the top of the page.

"You spoke to a John Malone recently," Otis said. "What was that conversation about?"

"You're serious," Simon said. "What's going on?"

"Malone was murdered. His death was staged to look like an accident."

Simon was so stupefied he couldn't respond for a few moments. He had convinced himself Malone's death had been an accident, but here was proof that his earlier suspicions were justified.

"We have no idea why," Otis said, reading Simon's face. "We're interviewing anyone who saw him recently. Phoebe Hays told us about your visit."

"How do you know Malone was murdered?"

"You answer my inquiries first, then I'll think about whether or not I should answer yours."

Simon could tell Otis was irritated with him for popping up in the midst of another homicide investigation. Simon could just imagine how angry he would be if he knew about the baby's corpse he and Morgan had disinterred, the corpse Simon knew existed because of an attractive woman's so-called past-life memories, which aforesaid pretty woman he'd been trying, in his own gentle way, to lure into his bed. What a mess.

"Sure, of course, ask away."

"What were you talking to Malone about?"

"I'm helping a friend, Helen Williams, do

some research on her family," Simon said. "A relative of hers was a matron at the old Raleigh Christian Orphanage. Malone knew the woman, first at the Orphanage, then later when they worked for the same family, the Grimes family."

"Really," Otis said. "I'm surprised that a Pulitzer Prize–winning professor such as yourself would get involved with a genealogy project. Isn't this exam week?"

"Helen is Wade Ferrell's goddaughter," Simon said, thinking fast. "She found evidence that implies this ancestor of hers killed someone. It's worried her terribly, caused her a lot of psychological problems, so Wade asked me to help her find out the truth."

Otis didn't say anything immediately. He sat and stared at Simon, tapping his pen on his notebook.

Simon felt a trickle of perspiration run down his spine and his face flush. He felt guilty because he was concealing the truth from Otis. Oh, he hadn't told a lie exactly, but he was walking down a very narrow path between truth and falsehood. Trying to protect Morgan and Helen, yet answer everyone's questions truthfully, was becoming difficult. If Otis ever found out about his dissembling, not only would their friendship implode, but Otis wouldn't hesitate to arrest him and charge him with obstruction of justice. There was getting to be too much at stake here for Simon's comfort.

Otis finally spoke. "Murder in the distant past," he said. "Now I understand your interest. You know, Simon, you have a habit of stirring up trouble when you investigate these antique murders that fascinate you so much. Mostly because you leave the trained professionals, the police, that is, in the dark for too long."

"I don't know there was a murder," Simon said. "That's what we're trying to find out."

"How long ago was this?"

"About a hundred years."

"Do you think Malone's death had anything to do with your investigation?"

"I doubt it. Surely he would have been murdered before I talked to him, not after, if that was the case."

Otis clicked his pen shut and replaced his notebook in his jacket pocket.

Thank God, Simon thought. He reassured himself that only he and David Morgan knew about the baby's corpse, and Morgan certainly wouldn't tell anyone. Morgan would die on the rack before admitting he'd violated the state human remains statute.

"Your turn," Simon said. "How do you know Malone was murdered?"

"He had a crater in the back of his skull he couldn't have gotten falling down a flight of stairs," Otis said. "Then there's the blood and bone adhering to his wife's bowling ball, which was wrapped in a black garbage bag and buried in a compost heap behind the garage. And though Malone stunk of bourbon, his blood alcohol content was negligible. Apparently the guy always enjoyed a toot when his wife was out of town, but he was expecting her the afternoon he died, so he hadn't had a drink since the night before. The killer dribbled a shot of bourbon on Malone's corpse so it would look like he was drunk."

"You don't suspect someone who lived in the main house, do you?"

"The family, Phoebe and her husband and Lucius and his wife and children, all alibi each other, but you know what that's worth. We're guessing the murder took place about five in the morning. Malone was fully dressed. Phoebe Hayes says he was an early riser. Anyone could have sneaked into Malone's apartment from the alley entrance to the garage. When you talked to Malone, did you meet the Hays family?"

"Oh, yes," Simon said. "I've met Phoebe and Lucius."

"You know Lucius is running for the Senate."

"So I hear."

"He found the body on his way to some power breakfast. The Hays family is pressuring us to close the case quickly."

"I can imagine."

"I don't know which is more important to them, keeping Lucius' name out of the newspaper relative to a murder, or finding a killer who did his business within yards of their house. I rather think the former."

For an hour after Otis left, Simon couldn't stop pacing. Stretching his imagination as far as it could go, and that was a long way, he couldn't connect Annie, or Helen, with any motive that anyone might have had to kill John Malone. Malone was an old family factotum. A Grimes family retainer, you might say. Could Malone know something about Annie that would reflect badly on Stella's descendants? Was Simon's poking around in their past somehow a threat to the family? But Annie lived a hundred years ago — what could she have done that would matter to anyone except Helen? Then there was Miss Henly's questionable death. When he and Helen had visited her, she didn't seem despondent or in pain. Anyone could have visited her the afternoon of her death without being noticed. He'd almost mentioned Miss Henly's death to Otis, but decided to wait for the results of her post-mortem before dragging her demise into the mix. Surely he was being paranoid, and her death was a coincidence. The woman was ninety-seven years old. At her age, she could have had some kind of stroke and taken all her pills without realizing what she was doing.

Simon called Helen.

"Did I wake you?" he asked.

"Not at all. I've been trying to sleep, but I can't. I just keep staring at the ceiling, thinking about Annie."

"Me, too. Let's do something constructive. Let's go to Fuquay-Varina and look for church records."

"I'm with you. Be ready in five minutes."

"I'll be there in six."

Rural North Carolina, in all its unzoned glory, flanked NC 401 South all the way from Raleigh to Fuquay-Varina. Soybean and tobacco fields hibernating for the winter, murky farm ponds, and deep woods alternated with brick ranch houses and double-wide trailers, and churches with backlit signs displaying the title of Sunday's sermon. An abandoned automobile detail shop, sheathed in rusty corrugated metal, sat next door to a beautifully restored two-story colonial farmhouse nestled in expensive landscaping. A compound of farm bungalows, all single-story, with squat pillars holding up wide porches, was surrounded by enough cars to fill an apartment building parking lot. A farm supply store festooned with lights and wreaths advertised Christmas trees and home-crafted decorations for sale. American flags flew everywhere. At the highway crossing with Ten-Ten Road, For Sale signs pointed the way to several new bedroom communities. A shopping center with a Wal-Mart, a grocery store, and the typical fast-food restaurants, was being built in one corner of the intersection. A *tienda,* advertising Mexican groceries and movies, and reflecting the influx of Hispanic immigrants, resurrected a decrepit single-pump gas station.

As they drew near Fuquay-Varina, strip malls and fast-food places appeared, then gave way to the town's historic district.

"This is lovely," Helen said. "I'd live there without a problem," she said, pointing toward a Federal mansion painted pale green, surrounded by wide verandas, with several brick chimneys, and about a half acre of landscaped grounds. A white Colonial-Revival house with a Doric portico and about a dozen tall columns stood across the street, and more houses in Craftsman and late-Victorian styles lined the street as they followed it downtown.

"Fuquay-Varina used to be two towns, obviously," Simon said. "Fuquay Springs attracted money early because of the mineral springs found here and the resort industry that followed. People came from all over to 'take the cure.' "

"Annie's obituary mentioned that she once worked in a hotel here."

"Oddly, Varina, which grew up just across the railroad tracks, was a mill town. It had tobacco warehouses, a cotton mill, and a big train depot. Completely different identity. The towns merged in the early sixties."

"Do you know where the church is?"

"Got directions off the Internet."

Simon pulled into the parking lot of the old church.

"No way this church is a hundred years old," he said.

"But the sign says Fuquay Memorial Methodist Church," Helen said.

"I know. But it's not the original church.

If the early church burned, as many did, the records may have gone with it."

"Don't even think that."

The modest church, built of worn brick that needed repointing, trimmed in fresh white paint, with a humble entrance, barely arched windows and doors, and no steeple, was, Simon guessed, about seventy-five years old. It was surrounded by even older millhouses adapted for modern use, with car sheds in the back and satellite dishes on the roofs. Simon tried the main door of the church, then the side door. Both were locked.

Helen, frustrated, jiggled the doorknob.

"Now what," she said.

"I believe," Simon said, "that house over there may be the parsonage."

Behind the church was a modest home built of the same brick as the church and trimmed with the same bright white paint. They crossed its yard, decorated with a homemade crèche jigsawed out of plywood and painted in bright primary colors, obviously by the Sunday School children. The faces of Joseph, Mary, and Jesus were contrived from pictures photocopied from art books, pasted on the holy family's heads, and varnished until they shone.

A well-padded middle-aged white woman

answered the door. The odor of baking sugar cookies wafted past her, making Simon's stomach growl.

"I saw you trying to get into the church," she said. "We have to keep it locked, I'm sorry to say, to keep the vagrants out."

"We wondered if we could talk to the pastor," Simon said.

"He's my husband," she said, wiping her hands on a dishtowel tucked into her apron, then extending her right hand. "His name is Jerome Wilson. I'm Mandy. He's not here right now, he's visiting a parishioner at the hospital. You could come back around two, then he's sure to be here."

"We'll do that," Simon said. "But let me ask one thing. Is this the church that was founded here in 1903?"

"Same church, different building. The original church burned in 1931."

"Do you know if any records exist from that time?"

"Oh, yes," she said. "We have all the old registers and the original church Bible. They're in my husband's office. He'd love to show them to you."

Helen and Simon had to kill time until two o'clock.

"Hungry?" Simon asked.

"I could eat," she said.

"Look for a place with a lot of pickups out front."

On a whim, Simon took a side street and wound up on the fringes of town, where he found a pink cinderblock building with Darryl's BarBQ written over the door.

"Lots of pickups here," Helen said.

A bell over the door tinkled as they walked in. They sat down at the last remaining table by a window that looked over the parking lot. Inside the restaurant was painted bright yellow, with green-checked curtains at the windows.

They barely had time to look over the menu before a waitress came to take their order. She tugged a pencil from its perch in her dyed black bouffant hairdo.

"Decided, hon?" the waitress asked.

"I'll have the vegetable plate," Helen said. "Turnip greens, mashed potatoes, fried apples, and butter beans. Are the butter beans good?"

"They were fresh-picked when I froze them last summer, honey," she said.

After getting reassurance from the waitress that Darryl cut his own French fries and left the potato skins on, Simon ordered pork ribs, seasoned fries, and cole slaw.

Simon didn't realize how tired he was of

fancy party fare until he sank his teeth into the succulent ribs. The hush puppies and biscuits, spread with real butter, that came with their meal melted in his mouth.

They both cleaned their plates, then ordered coffee. Simon had a piece of lemon chess pie, minus a few bites shared with Helen.

"It's still just one o'clock," Helen said. "I'm so anxious to see those records, I don't know what I'm going to do for another hour."

Simon gestured for the waitress. She came over to them with her coffee jug to refill their mugs.

"Tell me," Simon said. "Are you from around here?"

"Not originally," she said. "I come from Dunn. But I married Darryl here twenty-seven years ago," she said, nodding at the man ringing up tickets at the cash register, "so I been here awhile."

"Have you ever heard of a family named Evans? My friend here is researching a relative named Evans, and we know they farmed here a hundred years ago."

The waitress cocked her hip toward the back of the room, and called out to an old man smoking a cigarette at a table near the kitchen door.

"Marvin," she called out, "these people want to talk to you about the old days!" She turned back to Helen and Simon. "Marvin's always ready to reminisce. His family settled their place back when Indians lived here."

Marvin made his way carefully to their table, hunched low over a metal cane, steadying himself as he went by grasping the backs of chairs with the other hand. Simon stood up quickly and pulled over a chair, then helped him sit down. Marvin, whom Simon guessed was in his late eighties, was dressed in an impeccably ironed white dress shirt, denim overalls, and work boots.

"What do you want to know?" Marvin asked.

"Want some more coffee, Marvin?" the waitress asked. "And how about some pie? These folks are paying." She telegraphed a significant look Simon's way.

"Please," Simon said. "Order whatever you like."

"Coffee, sure," he said, "and a piece of that molasses pie, please."

"How long have your people lived here?" Helen asked.

"Since it was called Sippihaw, after the Indians," Marvin said. "We used to farm, but not anymore. My boys all went into the military, then got jobs in Raleigh. Their children went to college. You know how it is."

"Did you ever know a couple named Evans?" Simon said. "Leonard and Annie Evans."

Marvin leaned back and pondered. "Not a Leonard Evans," he said. "I knew a Johnny Evans. Farmed off Old Powell Road. Used to help him sucker his tobacco. He didn't live on the place, because the house was gone. Lived in town. But you know, I think he inherited the farm from his older brother. That's right. There was a house fire, and the brother died."

"That sounds right," Helen said, consulting the copy of Annie's obituary she'd brought with them. "It says in Annie Evans' obituary that she had taken a job after her husband died because his brother got the property."

"That was the way things worked back then. Want to know where the farm was?"

"Yes, please," Helen said.

Marvin unfolded a heavy paper napkin and scrawled a map on it with Simon's pen. "You go way on out here," he said. "Maybe six miles. You'll see a falling-down tobacco barn on the left, and two new brick houses on the right. You can't miss it. Then you go on down this old road here, and you should get to the place. I think the chimney's still standing."

They left Marvin slowly and deliberately eating his pie, as if it might be his last piece.

The house, or its remains, was right where Marvin said it would be. A fieldstone chimney lay in a heap at one end of a charred stone foundation.

"Do you really think this is it?" Helen said.

"Sure," Simon said. "Marvin sounded like he knew what he was talking about to me."

Helen rested her hand on the stones of the chimney and closed her eyes.

"Feel any vibrations?" Simon asked.

Helen opened her eyes and laughed.

"No, and not any auras or spirits! And I don't recognize the place. I mean the location. All the outbuildings are gone, too."

Simon went back to his car, opened the trunk, and removed a metal detector.

"Borrowed this from my friend David Morgan's garage," he said. He turned on the device, and moved it over the ground around the chimney.

"What are you expecting to find?" Helen asked. "Something with Annie's name on it? That would be too easy, wouldn't it?"

"I'm just playing," Simon said. "I love these things."

The metal detector beeped, and Simon dropped to his knees. With his pocket knife, he dug out an old metal spoon with the bowl bent at an angle.

"See if you can conjure a ghost with this," he said, handing it to Helen, who'd come over and knelt beside him. She took the spoon in both hands, smiling.

"I don't know any conjuring words," she said. She closed her eyes and lifted the spoon over her head melodramatically.

"I'm not getting a damn thing," she said.

"No vibrations, auras, or permutations?" Simon said, smiling.

"Just a minute!"

"What?"

"My leg's falling asleep," she said, standing up. She stuck the spoon in her pocket. Simon watched her wander around the ruin as he continued to crisscross what would have been the interior of the house. The detector beeped again a couple of times, and he excavated a 1912 penny and a nail. Helen ignored the sound and the artifacts. If she were faking her story, Simon thought, wouldn't she pretend to recognize the spoon, or run over to look at his new discoveries? Instead, she behaved like a person who wasn't familiar with the old farmhouse site and who was well aware that the stuff he was digging up was just trash.

The wind whipped up a chill December breeze. Deceived by the afternoon sun, they'd left their jackets in the car.

"Let's go," Helen said. "It's almost two, isn't it?"

This time Pastor Wilson answered the door himself, shaking Simon's and Helen's hands in turn.

"Come on in," he said, "my wife told me to expect you. She's in the church doing the flowers with the altar guild, but she left us some Christmas cookies."

His front door opened into a small living room clogged with furniture and knick-knacks. A blue velveteen "suite" consisting of a sofa, two chairs, and a recliner, faced a cheery fire. Over the mantel hung a really awful oil painting of Jesus standing in a fishing boat casting his net, either for fish or for sinners, depending on your religious persuasion. Angels were scattered everywhere: Needlework angels protected the arms of the chairs. Porcelain angels crowded tables. Any kind of angel that could accommodate a hook hung from the

Christmas tree crammed into the only available corner.

"I know it's a busy time of year for you," Simon said. "Thanks for seeing us."

"Did your wife tell you why we're here?" Helen asked.

"Come into my study," Pastor Wilson said. He led them into a tiny room where a plate of iced sugar cookies waited for them on a corner of his desk.

"Here," Pastor Wilson said, hauling a heavy leather church registry out of the bottom drawer of his desk. "I love looking through this myself. Who are you looking for?"

"Evans," Simon said. "Annie Evans. Moffat was her maiden name. Our information is that she was born in 1888, and married a Leonard Evans in June of 1906."

"The church didn't exist in 1888, so let's look for the entry for her marriage," Wilson said, carefully turning the pages of the book.

"Here it is," he said.

Simon and Helen crowded around him. Written there, in a beautiful hand, was the entry "Annie Moffat to Leonard Ames Evans, united in holy matrimony, June 11, 1906."

"And here," Wilson said, "is the baptism

of their child, Mary Alice Evans, on August 5, 1908."

"Are you sure?" Simon asked. "We didn't know they had a baby."

"Parents' names are Leonard and Annie Evans," Wilson said. "Uh, oh, the husband died not too long after that. Here's his funeral, in January 1909."

"He died in a fire," Simon said.

"What about the baby girl?" Helen asked. "Is her funeral recorded?"

"No," Wilson said, carefully turning more pages. "She must have survived the fire. Would you like copies of these pages?"

"Please," Simon said.

He looked over at Helen while the pastor made copies at a small desk-top copier. She looked almost as if she were in shock, gray-faced and dazed.

"Annie died in 1960," Simon said. "Was she buried here, do you know?"

The pastor consulted what he called the "cemetery book" to locate Annie's grave.

"Here," he said, handing Simon a cemetery map with a grave circled. "The graveyard's across the road."

Helen followed him like a robot to the pastor's front door, letting Simon make all the appropriate small talk. Simon took her hand as they waited for a break in traffic to allow them to cross the street.

"She had a baby girl," Helen said, resting a hand on Annie's gravestone. It was inscribed simply "Annie Moffat Evans, 1888–1960."

"I know," Simon said.

"The child she buried," Helen said. "And killed."

"You don't know that," Simon said.

"If she was widowed with a child, and her husband's brother inherited the farm, she might have been destitute. Would anyone have employed her if she had a child? Would the Orphanage have hired her?"

"Probably not. But that doesn't mean she killed her baby. There are other possibilities."

"Her obituary says she didn't have any children. And she wouldn't have needed to bury a child secretly if the child had died a natural death."

"The baby may have died of natural causes before Annie went to the Orphanage."

"Why isn't there a record of her death in the church register?"

"Dear girl, you're asking me questions I can't answer."

"Everything I remember about Annie's

life has turned out to be true."

"I know."

"Simon," she said.

"Yes?"

"My doll's name was Mary Alice. And she has blond hair and blue eyes. I picked her out myself, for my eighth birthday. She's sitting on my dresser, at home, right now."

Simon, for once in his life, couldn't find words.

Helen leaned toward him, and he reached out to her, pulling her into his arms. Tears dripped down her cheeks while Simon comforted her, stroking her hair.

"This isn't what was supposed to happen," Helen said. "You were supposed to find out Annie didn't exist."

"I'm so sorry," Simon said.

"I don't feel well," Helen said. "I want to go now."

Helen slept in the car on the way home, exhausted. Simon was worn out, too, buffeted by the emotions whipped up by worrying about Helen and closing in on Annie's history. They'd found Annie's records and where had it gotten them? Helen was convinced that she had murdered her own child almost a hundred years ago. Simon was close to the same conclusion. Then he forced his mind to stop churning. Evidence, he admonished himself. What are the facts? What information can I separate from coincidence to support our conclusions? It would be a huge step for the two of them to accept reincarnation. It embarrassed Simon just to think about it. How did historians who believed in reincarnation function? Verify their sources through a medium? Even worse were the psychological ramifications for Helen. What would her life be like if she believed herself to be a murderer?

Simon reviewed all the information he had collected since the moment Helen walked into his office looking for his help. Bit by bit and item by item, he isolated every scrap and mentally tortured it. Two streets before he turned into Helen's motel parking lot, a burst of intuition linked a few random comments, and he isolated one tiny clue. It gave him a glimmer of hope that he could relieve Helen's burden. Before he could offer Helen that hope though, he had a lot of work to do.

Simon gently shook Helen awake in front of the main door to the motel.

"Are we there already?" she asked.

"You've been asleep," he said. "Are you hungry? We missed dinner."

"I couldn't possibly eat."

"Look, I'm concerned about leaving you alone."

Helen smiled at him and squeezed his arm.

"We didn't learn anything today that I wasn't already afraid of. I can handle it. I've been living with Annie for years."

"This is different."

"You go home and get some sleep yourself. I'll have a glass of wine, maybe two, and read something until I get sleepy again. I'll get through the night okay."

"I've got a perfectly good guest bedroom."

"Good night, Simon." She leaned over and kissed him on the cheek.

"I'll call you in the morning, and we'll talk about what to do next," Simon said.

"What's left to do?"

Simon didn't tell her all his plans.

"We can look for evidence of Mary Alice Evans' life, find out if she lived past infancy. If she did, we'll know Annie didn't murder and bury her."

"Whatever you say. Really, I'm all right. Go on home."

Back in his home office, Simon searched online for a death notice for Mary Alice Evans, born on May 7, 1908 in Sippahaw,

North Carolina. He couldn't find one. Which meant what? That the girl had grown up, married, lived to be an old woman, and died a natural death under a married name? Perhaps her mother had given her up for adoption? Or left her with relatives so she could work? Or had she died as an infant of natural causes? But if she'd died under normal circumstances, why wasn't her death recorded in the church's register? Why would her mother bury her secretly in Oakwood Cemetery? How could Helen know a child was buried there if she didn't do it herself, in a previous life? How could it be a coincidence that Helen's doll was named Mary Alice? Enough coincidences became probability. He hoped that the single lonely clue he'd isolated in the car on the way home from Fuquay-Varina could lead to answers to all these questions.

Simon's head throbbed. He went downstairs and dissolved two Goody's Powders in an ice cold Coke, then lifted his telephone receiver and called Fred Grimes in Florida. They had a lengthy conversation.

"It's a long shot, son," Fred said. "But I agree with you. This is a question that demands an answer, whatever the consequences. I'll do everything in my power to help you learn the truth."

* * *

The next morning early Simon drove to Otis' office at police headquarters. If there was any possibility of a connection between Henly's "suicide," Malone's death, and Helen's quest, Otis needed to know about it. Simon would, of course, omit references to Helen's "past life" and his own violation of the Burial and Human Skeletal Remains Protection Act, the penalty for which was a fine and up to two years in prison. He'd looked it up.

Simon knocked on the doorframe of Otis' cubicle in the homicide division. Otis had his telephone to his ear, but when he saw Simon, he cradled the receiver.

"I was just dialing your number," Otis said. "Sit."

Simon sat.

"I've been thinking about our conversation yesterday," Simon began.

"Me, too," Otis said. "A report from the forensics lab about the lock from the storage unit where you and Helen Williams were trapped has found its way to my desk."

"And?"

"The lock was sabotaged. Someone injected it with instant glue."

"You're joking."

"No."

"We could have died there."

"Can you think why someone would do that?"

"No," Simon said. "I really can't. Unless it's related to something about the Grimes family I've dug up in my research. Or might dig up."

"Like what?"

"I have no idea," Simon said, truthfully. "And I came here this morning to tell you about another possible homicide."

After Simon finished his story, Otis called his watch commander for an update on the investigation into Lorena Henly's death. When he hung up he looked concerned.

"Official opinion on Miss Henly's death is mixed right now. The preliminary toxin scan verifies she died of a drug overdose, whether self-inflicted or not is unclear. Suicide would be the obvious inference, considering she had cancer, but the investigating officer is bothered by something he noticed at the scene."

"What?"

"Her sleeping medications were formulated in capsules. It seems that each capsule was opened, and the contents mixed in with ice cream, which she then consumed. But the capsule casings themselves, they'd been flushed down the toilet. One was found on the floor near the bowl."

"So?"

"If she committed suicide, why would she open all the capsules? Why not just take them? And why try to dispose of the casings?"

Simon pulled out his cell phone and called Helen. He told her a short version of what had happened. "Lock your door and don't let anyone in until I get there," Simon said.

"You two stay together and be careful," Otis said. "The Malone and Henly deaths may have nothing to do with you, probably don't, in fact, but someone for sure trapped you in that storage unit. You work on figuring out who and why and call me if you have any ideas. And please remember for once you're not a real detective."

Simon drove straight to Helen's hotel, then practically ran down the corridor to her room. He knocked on her door.

"What's the password?" Helen asked, from inside.

"Not funny," Simon said.

"I know it's not," Helen said, opening the door and beckoning him inside. "Just trying to lighten the mood. I'm worried sick."

"Me, too."

"I'm so sorry I got you into this," she said. "And John Malone. And Lorena Henly. And the Grimes family, for that matter. Simon, why would anyone trap us inside that storage unit? What's going on?"

"I don't know," Simon said. "But we're going to find out. Come on."

"Where are we going?"

"To the airport, to pick up Fred Grimes. His flight from Florida is due in half an hour."

11

> I think a rational person, if he wants, can believe in reincarnation on the basis of the evidence.
>
> — DR. IAN STEVENSON

For a ninety-one-year-old man, Fred Grimes was in mighty good shape. He was thin, slightly stooped, and walked with a decided limp, but he moved competently through the terminal exit and to Simon's waiting car at the curb, where Helen sat at the wheel to fend off prowling tow trucks. Grimes toted his own overnight bag, refusing Simon's offer to carry it for him. He was a handsome old man, with a full head of bright white hair and blue eyes framed with thick white eyebrows that almost, but not quite, met over his nose. He was impeccably dressed in black slacks, a sky blue silk polo shirt, and Gucci woven loafers. Before tossing his tote into the car trunk, he pulled a navy blue cashmere cardigan out of it and put it on against the chill air.

Grimes and Helen shared the passenger

seat of the T-bird, Helen moving as far as she could over toward the console, leaving Simon just enough room to shift gears.

Grimes turned to Helen and stretched out his hand in greeting.

"Funny," Grimes said. "You don't look a hundred years old."

"You told him," Helen said to Simon, clenching her jaws and narrowing her eyes.

"I had no choice," Simon said.

"Professor Shaw had to make a strong case to get me here," Grimes said. "But don't worry, your secret's safe with me. I've kept plenty in my life."

Helen didn't answer.

The Thunderbird moved out into the traffic, maneuvering around rental cars, shuttle buses, and jaywalkers lugging crammed suitcases and shopping bags overflowing with brightly wrapped Christmas gifts.

They stopped in front of the building that housed the offices of the Raleigh Christian Foundation and the Grimes Family Trust.

"Be back in a flash," Grimes said, climbing out of the car and going into the building.

"What's going on?" Helen asked. "What's he doing?"

"Wait and see," Simon said.

A few minutes later, Grimes came out of the building carrying a framed picture. He held it up against his chest so Helen couldn't see it as he got back into the car.

"Fred has a photograph to show you," Simon said to Helen. "Let's see if you recognize it."

"Another test?" Helen said, smiling at Simon, forgiving him for blowing her cover.

Grimes handed the picture over to Helen.

"Why, this is the house at Kerr Lake my parents rented," Helen said. "We stayed there for a couple of summers. My grandmother lived with us at the time, and it was too hot for her in Wilmington. But I don't understand. Why do you have a picture of it?" she asked Grimes.

"I owned it. With my sister Stella. It was our summer place."

Helen digested Grimes' words.

"Oh, my God," she said, gripping the frame. "That's the connection."

"You see," Grimes said. "After Stella died, in 1980, the family rarely used it. Phoebe and her husband bought a fancy place at Emerald Isle. I sold the house in 1987, but until then I rented it out every summer."

"Fred kept good records," Simon said. "Your parents rented the place during the summers of 1982 and 1983. You would have been seven and eight years old."

"Your friend Professor Shaw has a sharp memory," Grimes said. "He saw this photograph in the office, and remembered you'd mentioned spending summers at a house on Kerr Lake."

"It was a couple of days before I made the connection," Simon said. "I wish it had occurred to me earlier."

"I admit that the house links me with your family, but how does Annie Evans fit in?"

"After she retired, Annie lived in the house for years. She was living there when she died in 1960."

"Okay," Helen said, "that's weird, no doubt about it. But Annie died more than twenty years before I vacationed in that house. That doesn't explain why I have her memories. And what does all this have to do with John Malone's murder?"

"I don't know," Simon said. "But I'm sure they're linked."

"If it's a coincidence, it's a mighty big one," Grimes said.

"Everything Fred saved from that house is in Phoebe Hays' attic," Simon said. "And we're going to sift through every scrap of it for clues."

"Phoebe said we couldn't," Helen said.

"The deed to that house is in my name," Grimes said. "Besides, Phoebe and Lucius and the rest of the family went to New York, to shop for Christmas and to visit my son and his family. They go every year about now. They won't bother us."

Simon parked behind the Hays mansion. They had to skirt the garage on the way to the back door of the house, so they couldn't miss the yellow crime scene tape wrapped around the staircase. Or the dark stain on the concrete at the foot of the stairs.

Grimes stared at the bloodstain, then looked up at the stairs.

"This makes me angry," Grimes said. "John was a good man. Oh, he'd gotten grumpy and cantankerous, but that was old age and arthritis talking. He was church-going, hard-working, and the soul of discretion."

Grimes opened the back door with his key.

"Come on in," he said. "Make yourselves at home. I'll start some coffee."

Grimes led them into a vast kitchen that gleamed with stainless steel. He rummaged around in a pantry the size of Simon's kitchen, found coffee and sugar, and dumped the coffee into a fancy coffeemaker that had more levers and dials than the space shuttle.

"My suite on the second floor is much cozier than this, but I cleaned out my kitchen before I left for Florida," Grimes said. "Phoebe, on the other hand, is always prepared to entertain dozens of guests."

Grimes opened the refrigerator side of the double refrigerator-freezer and took out cream and a box of muffins.

"I'm starving," he said, "I didn't eat anything before I got on the plane."

The three of them sat at the kitchen table and drank their coffee and ate all the muffins off fine bone china so thin it made Simon a little nervous to handle it. Then Simon distributed more antihistamines, dust masks, and white cotton gloves. Grimes sorted through a junk drawer and found a pair of scissors and a utility knife.

"I boxed up some of that stuff good," he said. "Let's go." Helen and Simon followed Grimes out into a hall. Grimes opened a door for them.

"The attic must be four flights up in this house," Simon said.

"It is," Grimes said, grinning. "But we don't have to take the stairs."

He guided them into an elevator concealed behind the paneled door, then pushed the appropriate button. They whooshed upward. The elevator door opened at the head of a narrow set of stairs in front of an old pine door.

Grimes opened the door and led them into a vast attic.

"Wow," Helen said. "Imagine what all this stuff would go for on eBay!"

"I'm the original pack rat," Grimes said. "I save everything. I don't know why. When I go to glory, Phoebe will probably just dump it all at the Goodwill store."

The attic had to be three-thousand-square feet, thought Simon. Furniture, trunks, and boxes crammed the main room. Several side rooms opened off the main space. It was a little chilly, but not too cold to work. As if reading Simon's mind, Grimes went to a thermostat and turned the heat up.

"I had the attic insulated and HVAC added when I bought the house," Fred said. "There's no reason to keep all this stuff just to let it be ruined."

"I can't imagine what your electric bill is," Simon said.

"Don't you worry," Fred said, laughing. "I can afford it."

"My mother kept boxes of our books in

our attic," Helen said. "She said they collected too much dust on bookshelves. Over the years the insects and mold got to them. My grandmother left me all three volumes of *Kristen Lavransdatter*, in pristine condition. They were ruined."

"I've got something special to show you," Fred said. The trio picked their way around a couple of old steamer trunks strapped with leather and secured with brass locks, a heavy Edwardian sideboard, and a child's mahogany trundle bed until they reached one of the side rooms. Grimes ceremoniously flung the door open, bowing Helen inside.

"Ohmigod! Books!" Helen said, as she almost ran inside.

"I kept these in the house at Kerr Lake for my children and grandchildren to read during the summers," Fred said.

"An original set of the Bobbsey Twins!" Helen said. "And all the Black Stallion books! And look, *Hans Brinker and the Silver Skates*! And *Kidnapped*, with N.C. Wyeth's original illustrations!"

Helen moved along the shelves, exclaiming with delight over each new discovery.

"You act like you've found Blackbeard's treasure," Simon said.

"Better than that," Helen said. "You know what," she said to Grimes, opening the pages of a gilt-edged leather-bound copy of *The Wind in the Willows*. "I believe I read most of these at your lake house."

"I wouldn't be surprised. I left a note on the bookcases telling all the tenants to enjoy the books, as long as they took care of them," Grimes said.

Simon knelt on the floor, examining a set of encyclopedias.

"This is the 1911 Britannica, supposedly the best encyclopedia ever written," Simon said. "With the 1922 and 1926 supplements. The full set is almost impossible to find. It's worth a fortune."

"There's not a children's book here about an orphanage matron, is there?" Helen said.

"Sorry," Fred said. "That would be too easy, I'm afraid."

"Okay, guys, we've had enough fun," Simon said. "We could spend days playing up here. Remember, we're looking for anything of Annie's." Simon pulled on his gloves.

"Like what?" Grimes asked.

"The trunk full of her personal effects you can't remember what you did with. A shoe box full of letters. Scrapbooks. Housekeeping records. Look at everything. And try not to get distracted."

"I believe," Helen said, pulling on her gloves and flexing her fingers. "I'll work in this room."

"Oh no," Simon said, turning her around and pushing her gently toward the door. "You can't be trusted with this many books. You'd start reading, and we'd find you years later, mummified."

"Come with me, Helen," Grimes said. "I saw a desk that was in the house when Annie lived there. Let's go rummage through the drawers. If I remember correctly, it's got about a dozen secret compartments."

Simon waited until Grimes and Helen were well into the other room before he started his search, methodically, with the first volume on the top shelf of the bookshelf nearest the door. "Please, Lord," he whispered. "It's Christmas, remember?"

An hour or so later Simon left the book room and found Helen and Fred burrowing into a steamer trunk.

"Would you look at this?" Helen said, holding up a black lace corset. "Do you believe women wore these things? And look at these shoes," she said, showing him a pair of black lace-up heels. "Imagine how long it took to get dressed every day? Not to mention the heat in summer."

"My father's World War I uniform is here," Grimes said. "It's in good shape, thanks to Phoebe's devotion to scattering mothballs and mouse poison. I'm thinking I should donate a lot of this to the Raleigh City Museum. What do you say, Simon? Think they'd be interested?"

Simon didn't answer. He pulled off his filthy gloves and sat down on a nearby chair. Helen noticed a thin volume tucked under his arm.

"What have you got there?" she asked.

"What I was hoping to find," Simon said.

The blood drained from her face. Even though she was kneeling, she swayed a bit. Grimes took her arm, and Simon unscrewed the cap of a bottle of water and handed it to her.

"Drink," he said.

Helen drank, then sat on the floor, crossing her legs. Grimes joined her, knees popping audibly as he stretched out his legs in front of him.

"Tell me?" she asked.

"I found Annie Evans' diary," Simon said.

"Let me see it," Helen said, stretching out her hand.

Simon didn't give it to her.

"Now," she said. "Hand it over."

"For God's sake, give it to her," Grimes said. "She's waited long enough."

"Wait five minutes, let me explain," Simon said.

Helen crossed her arms and sat in silence, waiting.

"Annie was a Victorian woman," Simon said. "She would have kept a memory book. She didn't do a good job of it, mind you. There are just a few entries."

"I want to see it," Helen said.

"I think that when Annie died," Simon went on, "someone picked this volume up from her room, and, believing it was a book that belonged to the Grimeses, slipped it into the bookshelves. Or maybe Annie placed it there herself, who knows. Years later, a little girl who loved to read found it among the classics on the bookshelf of the summer place her family rented at Kerr Lake. A precocious reader, she devoured it along with most of the other books she discovered. But this book was different. It was the diary of a real person, Annie Evans, who worked as a matron for the Raleigh Christian Orphanage early in the century, then as housekeeper for the family who owned the lake house."

Helen drew her knees up to her chest,

wrapped her arms around her knees, and dropped her head onto them.

"I don't believe it," she said, her voice muffled.

Fred Grimes patted her gently on the shoulder.

"Among other more ordinary events, the diary recorded a terrible fire and the burial of a child's corpse. The scary entries conjured up visual images and impressions that the little girl couldn't forget. She must have realized that the diary wasn't a story book, that the life it recorded was real. Over time, she came to believe that these memories were her own. Psychologists call it . . ."

Helen raised her head. "I know," she said. "Cryptoamnesia. I've read enough about it. It's happens when an individual forgets learned information and it reappears later as constructed memory," she recited. "In other words, I forgot that I got Annie's stories from her diary. I had no idea false memories could feel so real."

She burst into sobs, and dropped her head back onto her knees. Simon and Fred both reached out to comfort her.

"Don't touch me," she said. "Leave me alone." They didn't leave her; both men sat quietly by her side. Simon's eyes met Fred's. They showed only sympathy for

Helen. He hadn't yet realized how this discovery might affect him.

Helen's sobs subsided. She raised her head and wiped her face. Fred handed her a clean handkerchief he produced from his pocket, and she rubbed it over her face.

"I'm a fool and an idiot," she said.

"No, you aren't," Simon said. "Not at all. You were a little girl, very disturbed by what you read in this diary. They were real memories. They just weren't yours. The questions the diary raised troubled you. As you grew up, you assumed the memories yourself. It could happen to anyone."

"Sure," Helen said. "Anyone."

"Children personify everything. They think what they read in books or see on a movie screen is happening to them. That's why we shield children from graphic violence and sex. They can't objectify it."

"Let me see the book," Helen said.

"Let's look through it together," Simon said.

"Why don't we go downstairs where we can be comfortable?" Grimes asked. "It's getting late. I'll make us some more coffee and find something to eat."

"Coffee would be good," Helen said, "if you add something stronger to it. Like bourbon."

"I can do that," Grimes said.

Once downstairs, Grimes showed them to a small study near the kitchen. It was furnished with leather sofas and photographs of Phoebe and Lucius with various Republican luminaries, including Senator Elizabeth Dole and the second President Bush. Fred lit the gas fire and went off to make coffee. Simon and Helen waited for him to come back before going through the diary. Helen stared at the fire while Simon worried about her.

Shortly, Grimes returned with a silver tray crowded with food and drink. He handed out mugs of coffee spiked with bourbon. Crab cakes, spring rolls, ham biscuits, and chicken wings filled a plate. Another held a selection of bite-size pastries.

"Let me guess," Simon said. "Party leftovers."

"Found them in the freezer," Grimes said. "Nuked them in the microwave."

Helen sipped at her coffee but didn't touch the food.

"Ready?" Simon asked.

"Sure," she said. "Why not?"

Simon sat between the two of them and turned the pages of the book.

"Annie wasn't a committed diary keeper," Simon said. "She just occasionally wrote an entry. But there's more than enough tragedy recorded here to disturb a little girl with a powerful imagination."

"Here," he said, showing them the first entry, "this is Annie's description of the fire that killed her husband. She didn't anticipate anyone else ever reading this, so she didn't bother to name people or dates or explain anything. She just recorded her experiences."

He turned more pages. "She must have liked Christmas, because she mentions several. Here she describes a new checked skirt she wore one Christmas Eve, and another time she writes that Stella gave her an embroidered handkerchief. She records her anger about the Orphanage boys holding a bug funeral one summer. She talks about walking the neighborhood next to the Orphanage to visit a special friend, and her disappointment that the grocery store was closed so she couldn't take a gift. And, of course, she describes the burial of the baby. Without telling us who she was or how she died."

"I want to read it," Helen said.

Simon handed her the volume.

She read it. It only took a few minutes.

"Everything's here," Helen said, "just as I visualized it. At least I know it wasn't me living in a past incarnation! What was I thinking?"

"There's a picture and a postcard tucked in the back," Simon said.

Helen withdrew them, and Grimes looked over her shoulder.

"The picture is of Stella, my sister," Grimes said. "We had that taken right after we retrieved her from the Orphanage." The girl was blond, with long curly hair tied up in a hair ribbon, light eyes looking calmly into the camera, wearing a high-collar lace dress. "I remember when we first met. She was eleven. She was the prettiest, sweetest girl. What an experience that was for a six-year-old boy! I put her on a pedestal right away, and never had cause to take her off it the rest of her life. I remember Stella wanted to give a copy of the photograph to Miss Annie."

Grimes passed the photograph to Helen.

"Then there's this," Simon said. He showed them a postcard labeled "Brevard House, on the Raleigh Christian Orphanage Campus" with a picture of the house where Helen had fainted a few days ago.

"It would have been helpful," Helen said, "if I'd remembered the caption on this postcard. I could have saved myself a lot of grief."

Helen's color crept back into her face. She put down her empty coffee mug and reached for a crab cake.

"I guess we'll never know who that baby was," Grimes said. "We don't really know it's even true, do we?" he said.

"It's true," Simon said. He steeled himself, then told them both about finding the baby's corpse.

"Quite an experience for you and your friend," Grimes said.

"You didn't tell me," Helen said. "You were trying to protect me."

"Yeah, I suppose I was," Simon said.

"It must have been her child," Helen said. "She must have murdered her. Because she had to get work after her husband died, and she couldn't do it with a baby, could she? Maybe she, and it, were starving. She might have had nowhere to go."

"I don't think so," Simon said.

"Do you have a different solution in mind?"

"Yes, but you should brace yourself," Simon said to Fred.

"What do you mean?" Grimes said.

"I mean that the baby in that grave, I believe it's your sister Stella."

Grimes stood up, clenching his fists.

"You bastard! How dare you! I came all

the way from Florida and let you paw around my things in my own house to hear this nonsense?"

"I'm sorry," Simon said. "I really am. More than I can say. But it's the truth. The photograph confirms it. Look," he said, showing the back of the photograph to Grimes.

Simon turned the picture of Stella over, and showed Fred and Helen the tiny writing, so faded it was almost illegible, at the bottom edge of the paper.

"I can't read it," Grimes said. "I don't have my reading glasses."

"It says 'Mary Alice, age eleven,' " Simon said.

"I don't believe you," Grimes said.

"It does, Fred," Helen said, taking the photograph from Simon and scrutinizing it.

Grimes went to a drawer and got a large magnifying glass. He examined the photograph minutely.

"So what?" he said. "The woman was fantasizing, that's all. She adored Stella. She wanted her to be her daughter. That's all."

"No," Simon said. "I'm afraid not. I think that Annie Evans boarded her child near the Orphanage, where she could visit her. You remember, Helen, her description of the houses on that street during her walk on that winter night? They were all widows, who might take in a baby to help pay the bills. She was on her way to visit the child."

"You're delusional yourself," Grimes said. He was still standing, gripping the edge of the desk so hard blue veins popped out on his hand.

"Then Stella came to the Orphanage," Simon said. "She became ill with measles and then pneumonia. Annie was immune, so she went into quarantine with Stella to care for her. But Stella died. So few children lived — there were no antibiotics, no intravenous fluids. Annie saw a way to have her own child with her. Both children were about eighteen months old, both were blond with blue eyes. Annie sneaked Stella's corpse out of the infirmary and buried it, then returned with Mary Alice, who passed as the miraculously cured Stella for the rest of her life."

"Why would she give up Stella, Mary Alice, whoever, to my family?" Grimes asked.

Simon shrugged. "For the child's own good," Simon said. "Your family was rich. Think of the advantages. Not to mention what might happen to Annie if she confessed."

"Is that what Annie wanted to tell Fred on

her deathbed?" Helen asked. "That Stella was Mary Alice Evans?"

"You can't be sure of any of this without a DNA test on that corpse," Grimes said. "And to get one, you and your archaeologist friend might have to go to jail. The way I feel about you right now, that wouldn't displease me."

"Oh, I know it's true, even without an exhumation," Simon said.

"How?" Grimes said.

"Because John Malone was murdered."

12

> If you're too open-minded, your brains will fall out.
>
> — ANONYMOUS SKEPTIC

The kitchen door slammed, hard. Grimes moved to call out, but Simon leaped to his feet, clapping a hand over Grimes' mouth, and shaking his head.

Grimes waited, quietly. Later he would say he didn't know why he obeyed Simon, as angry as he was with him, but he did.

Footsteps sounded through the kitchen and down the hall. The elevator door opened, then closed, and the lift mechanism engaged. They heard the elevator rising above them.

Grimes went to the study window, then turned back to Simon and Helen, looking relieved.

"It's Jesse's car," Grimes said. "I thought he'd gone to New York with the others, but apparently not."

Simon scanned the room.

"Where's the telephone?" he asked. "We

need to call the police."

"Didn't you hear me?" Grimes asked. "It's just Jesse, my great nephew."

"He's a dangerous man. He killed John Malone."

"That's absurd," Grimes said. "Why would he kill John?"

Simon spotted a telephone, tastefully hidden in a leather box on the desk, and reached for it.

"Stop it," Grimes said, grabbing the receiver from him and slamming it back into its cradle. "What's wrong with you? I'm going upstairs to see Jesse."

"Think a minute. Why is he here? He doesn't live here. I think he's gone up to the attic. He knows Helen and I wanted to search it, and he wants to beat us to it."

"That's not it, I'm sure," Grimes said. "He's just come to pick up something. He keeps a bedroom here."

"I'm telling you, we need to call the police."

"He hasn't done anything. Look, let's go on upstairs, I'll talk to him, clear everything up."

The three of them, Helen still toting the diary, went to the elevator.

"See," Simon said, pointing to the floor indicator. "He's in the attic."

"He can't be looking for the diary," Helen said. "No one knew it existed before today."

"He doesn't know what he's looking for," Simon said. "It's a long story, but believe me, we should call the police."

"Go ahead," Grimes said. "I'll have them arrest you instead for being a goddamned nuisance. I'm going upstairs to see what Jesse's doing. You'll see, he'll have a good reason to be here."

Simon gave in. Grimes was right, he had no firm evidence to implicate Jesse in Malone's murder. Jesse had a key to the house. He had every right to be here.

"Okay," Simon said. "But I'm going with you."

"Me, too," Helen said.

Grimes pushed the button for the elevator.

"You don't happen to have a gun around, do you?" Simon asked.

"Don't be ridiculous," Grimes said.

The three of them went up to the attic. Simon knew there'd be a nasty scene, but he didn't know how to avoid it. Grimes would never believe him otherwise.

The three of them surprised Jesse going through the drawers of a walnut dresser. He was dressed for searching in a tattered sweatshirt, jeans, and gloves.

"Hey, boy," Fred said, stretching out a hand to him. "What are you doing here?"

"Uncle Fred," Jesse said. "I could ask you the same thing. I didn't know you were in town." Jesse looked past Grimes and saw Simon and Helen. "Why are they here? Phoebe said she didn't want them poking around."

"What are you looking for, Jesse?" Simon asked, plopping down on a settee draped in a dust sheet. "Love letters?"

"Love letters? What are you talking about?" Grimes said.

"Your entire family, including Jesse, was tested for compatibility for a possible bone marrow match when Lucius' son Rick contracted leukemia, am I right?"

"Yeah," Grimes said. "What has that got to do with anything?"

"That's how Jesse found out he's not related to you or your children, Fred," Simon said. "Biologically, anyway."

"You self-righteous prig," Jesse said. "Why couldn't you just stay out of our family's business?"

"Oh my God," Fred said, looking at Jesse. "Of course."

"When Jesse learned his blood test didn't match any of the Grimes' results, Fred, he jumped to conclusions. I mean, what would anyone think? He figured that Joseph Lay wasn't his biological father. He assumed his mother had had an affair, didn't you, Jesse? What would happen if that got out? What would happen to your income from the Grimes trust?"

"Has anyone ever told you you're too smart for your own damn good?" Jesse said.

"Oh, yes," Simon said. "Many times."

Jesse drew a pistol from under his shirt and aimed it directly at Simon.

"Bad idea," Simon said to Jesse, crossing his legs and settling back into the settee. "Too many witnesses."

"Fred and I know everything," Helen said. "You can't kill all three of us. Not and get away with it."

Jesse hesitated, still aiming the gun at Simon, obviously itching to punish him. Helen slid the diary under a short stack of books on a nearby table.

"When you got those test results back, you couldn't ask your mother about them," Simon said. "She's dead. But then you figured, no one else could know, either. Then Helen and I started to poke around in your family history. You were worried what we might find out. Especially when we talked to John Malone. He'd been your family's chauffeur and trusted servant for years. He didn't like you much. Always told everyone you weren't anything like your father. You imagined the worst, that he knew you weren't Joe's son. Perhaps he'd driven your mother to an amorous rendezvous, or delivered messages to her lover. So you killed him."

"No," Jesse said. "I didn't. John fell down the stairs. The police said so."

"They found the murder weapon," Simon said. "You did a very poor job of hiding it."

"There was no reason for any of this, Jesse," Grimes said sadly. "It was Stella, your grandmother. She wasn't my sister, that's why we're not blood kin. But I don't care. I loved Stella, I'll always think of her as my sister. You're her only grandchild. I wouldn't dream of cutting you off."

Jesse stared at him. "Grandmother wasn't your sister? What are you talking about?"

"Annie Evans kept a diary," Fred said. "My sister died as an infant, and Annie exchanged her own daughter for her."

"We found the diary in the attic this morning," Helen said.

"As soon as we learned that your grandmother wasn't really Stella Grimes, I realized that her descendants wouldn't be related to Fred," Simon said. "Then I remembered the blood tests, and figured you'd found out you weren't a Grimes. But you didn't know why, and you guessed wrong. You killed John Malone to protect a secret he never had."

"You've got to believe me," Jesse said to his uncle. "I didn't mean to kill John. I was drunk. I'd been at a party all night. I stopped in to see him, to ask him about what he said to these two. You wouldn't believe how nasty he was to me. The way he talked, I thought he knew . . . well, I lost my temper, lashed out at him."

"With a bowling ball?" Simon said. "You've got quite a temper."

"Shut up," Jesse said.

Helen was furious. "You trapped us in that storage unit," she said. "We could have died in there."

"I just wanted to discourage you," Jesse said. "I wasn't trying to kill you."

"If we'd been locked in that room for days, without water or food, what do you think was going to happen to us?" Helen asked.

Jesse turned to his great-uncle. "Listen to me, Uncle Fred, I didn't mean . . ."

"Spare me the excuses," Fred said to Jesse. "You belong in prison. Give me that gun."

Jesse hesitated, desperate for a way out, his eyes roving from Fred to Simon to Helen and back to Fred.

"I might be able to get away, if you help me."

"Use your brains for once in your life," Fred said. "If you give yourself up, the district attorney might give you a break. I'll get you a good lawyer. I owe your grandmother that much."

Beaten, Jesse handed the gun to Grimes.

Simon didn't realize he was holding his breath until he exhaled with relief. Gently he took the gun from Grimes, who for the first time looked his age. Drained of energy, his unfocused eyes reflected shock and exhaustion. Simon felt for him. He'd been through a lot today.

Simon motioned Jesse toward the elevator.

"Let's go call Otis Gates," he said.

Before they left the attic, Helen retrieved Annie's diary and gave it to Fred.

"If this belongs to anyone, it belongs to you," she said. "It describes Stella's last days. Annie took good care of her."

Simon told Sergeant Gates the entire story, excluding Helen's initial claim of reincarnation, and his illegal grave-digging in

Oakwood Cemetery. The way he told it, he and Helen just stumbled coincidentally upon a century-old family secret, one so damaging that Jesse Lay was willing to kill John Malone to keep it quiet. Except the truth turned out to be different than Jesse thought.

"I guess we'll have to exhume this child's corpse and retrieve DNA to be sure she's Fred Grimes' sister. Are you positive there's a body there?"

"Oh yeah, I'm sure," Simon said.

"Your famous instincts," Otis said. "We'll need an expert to assist the coroner. Someone who will know if the corpse has ever been disturbed, if it was buried at the time the diary says, stuff like that."

Simon choked on his heart.

"Do you know when David Morgan will be back from Christmas vacation?" Otis asked. "He'd be the perfect guy to ask, don't you think?"

"Yeah," Simon said, feeling his heart settle back into its normal location. "He'd be perfect."

The days rolled pleasantly along toward Christmas. A cold front had moved in, raising the happy possibility of snow. Simon snagged the last half gallon of peppermint ice cream at the grocery store while harried husbands, cell phones to their ears, searched for the ingredients for Christmas dinner. "But, honey," Simon overheard one man plead, "I'm looking at the second shelf from the bottom, right side. There are no candied walnuts, I swear. Can I come home now?"

Simon was one of the hosts of a joint neighborhood Christmas party held across the street. Old people shuffled in on walkers or with canes, college students introduced new boyfriends and girlfriends, and everyone wore name tags to put first-timers at ease. Simon contributed a batch of potent eggnog served in his mother's silver punch bowl. Another host drove to the beach that morning and returned with bushels of fresh oysters. They built a fire outdoors and roasted the oysters, covered with wet burlap, on a piece of sheet metal over the open fire. Everyone, including children, stood around an outdoor bar and shucked the finished product, wearing thick rubber gloves to protect them from the sharp shells and oyster shuckers, dipping the tender little guys into melted butter or seafood sauce.

Later that night a motley band of carolers holding candles stuck through paper plates to catch the drips sang outside Simon's front door, accompanied by bells and a flute. They terrified the cats, who still huddled under the kitchen table an hour after the ordeal was over.

Late on Christmas Eve, Simon finished inserting fifty-dollar bills into envelopes to give to Marcus' daughters at dinner the next day. Marcus and his wife fussed at him for giving their daughters extravagant gifts, but he ignored them. What was the benefit of being the girls' honorary godparent if he couldn't spoil them?

He still needed to pack a bag before he went to bed. After dinner tomorrow, he was going straight to the airport to hop a plane to New York. His aunt and uncle were delighted that he'd get there in time for Friday night services. Leah knew the bass player at the Met, and scored tickets to *Moses und Aron* for the two of them and a girlfriend she wanted Simon to meet.

His telephone rang. "Helen" jumped into his mind. No, it wouldn't be her. They'd said good-bye several days ago. Simon had been resigned to her departure. No pining after inaccessible women for him. Moving on, that's what he was about. That's why he'd let Leah fix him up.

He answered the phone.

"Hello," Helen said. "Merry Christmas."

"Merry Christmas to you, too."

"Guess what Fred sent me?"

"The books."

"Yes, every single one in the attic library! With a note that said how sorry he was that I'd suffered so much anxiety because of his family. What a nice man."

"He gave me the 1911 Britannica. I'm up to Abraham." Simon's gift had arrived packed in expensive archival boxes, each volume wrapped in muslin.

"I deleted your e-mail by accident before I could read it, and I couldn't retrieve it. You've got to tell me everything right now."

She could have e-mailed him back and asked him to resend his message, but he was glad to hear from her. They'd shared an intense few days, and he missed her company.

"Let's see," Simon said. "Where should I start? Lorena Henly wasn't murdered. Her death was a coincidence. Jesse was working out at his health club when she died."

"Oh, thank God. What a relief. I feel responsible enough for everything else that's happened. So she killed herself?"

"With her sleeping pills. There weren't any opiates in her system, and her prescription for pain medication couldn't be refilled for two weeks. She must have been taking a lot more than directed. Maybe she ran out and thought she couldn't get more, or just accepted that it was her time. Her friends think she must have mixed the sleeping pills into her ice cream and tried to flush all the casings to make it appear she'd died naturally, thinking that her suicide would upset her friends."

"Poor woman."

"Oh, I don't know. She was ninety-seven and had a terminal illness. She made a decision. I'm not going to judge her."

"I assume the DNA test on the baby's corpse was positive, or I would have heard about it."

"The preliminary test showed a positive relationship to the Grimes family. The final report will take weeks to complete. The authorities aren't going to exhume the corpse in Stella's grave, or Annie. Fred objects, and the rest of the family wants the case closed as soon as possible. Before he went back to Florida, Fred came by and said he'd decided to inter the baby in the same grave as Stella/Mary Alice, and just leave the gravestone as it is for now."

"And Jesse?"

"He pled guilty to manslaughter one, on the assumption that he was very drunk and Malone baited him. He's allocuted to everything. Phoebe and Lucius are praying that the publicity from the case will settle down before the state Republican convention."

"I was sure Jesse would try to beat the rap."

"You do realize, if there had been a trial, we would've been witnesses, and we would've had to testify under oath?"

"I hadn't thought that far. We might have had to admit we were chasing disincarnate souls all over North Carolina! How embarrassing!"

"But not boring," Simon said.

Epilogue

On New Year's Eve, Simon and another dozen or so men in his neighborhood dragged discarded Christmas trees off the curbs and built a huge bonfire. In what had become an annual act of male-bonding, they warmed themselves in front of crackling flames and drank a lot of bourbon out of paper cups.

Before he went to bed that night, Simon sent an e-mail to the fifteen students preregistered for History 306, Historiography. *"The first meeting of my spring seminar on writing history,"* he wrote, *"will take place at the Village Draft House in Cameron Village Mall, at 6 p.m., January 4. Anyone who reveals the new location of the class to an unregistered student will be required to write a twenty-page paper on the topic of 'Literary Allusions in the Writings of Edward Gibbon.' Bring your IDs, I'm buying."*

About the Author

Sarah R. Shaber's first book, *Simon Said*, won the St. Martin's Press/Malice Domestic annual contest for the best first traditional mystery. Her next two books in the series, *Snipe Hunt* and *The Fugitive King*, were selections of the Mystery Guild Book Club. Shaber lives with her husband, son, and daughter in Raleigh, North Carolina, and can be reached at www.sarahshaber.com.

We hope you have enjoyed this Large Print book. Other Thorndike, Wheeler or Chivers Press Large Print books are available at your library or directly from the publishers.

For more information about current and upcoming titles, please call or write, without obligation, to:

Publisher
Thorndike Press
295 Kennedy Memorial Drive
Waterville, ME 04901
Tel. (800) 223-1244

Or visit our Web site at:
www.gale.com/thorndike
www.gale.com/wheeler

OR

Chivers Large Print
published by BBC Audiobooks Ltd
St James House, The Square
Lower Bristol Road
Bath BA2 3SB
England
Tel. +44(0) 800 136919
email: bbcaudiobooks@bbc.co.uk
www.bbcaudiobooks.co.uk

All our Large Print titles are designed for easy reading, and all our books are made to last.